"READING [...]
ARMCHAIR TR[...]

Alfred Hitchcock Mystery Magazine

A CASE OF VINEYARD POISON
A Martha's Vineyard Mystery

"THIS IS A GOOD ONE"
Chattanooga Times

"A DELIGHT . . .
Craig's style of writing is laid-back,
intelligent and fascinating.
His plots have become more complicated
and his characters more believable"

Copley News Service

"ONE OF THE MOST APPEALING AND
UNDERRATED WRITERS IN THE GENRE . . .
Craig is a consummate storyteller with a fluid style
and the skill to lure readers with his lifelike characters"

Murder & Mayhem

"LIKE SPENDING A DAY AT THE BEACH
WITH CLOSE, BANTERING FRIENDS . . .
Craig captains a pleasurable little junket
with his Martha's Vineyard crew."

Publishers Weekly

Martha's Vineyard Mysteries by
Philip R. Craig

A CASE OF VINEYARD POISON

A Martha's Vineyard Mystery

PHILIP R. CRAIG

AVON BOOKS
An Imprint of HarperCollins*Publishers*

AVON BOOKS
An Imprint of HarperCollins*Publishers*
10 East 53rd Street
New York, New York 10022-5299

Copyright © 1995 by Philip R. Craig
Published by arrangement with Scribner, an imprint of Simon & Schuster
Library of Congress Catalog Card Number: 94-39902
ISBN: 0-380-72679-3
www.avonbooks.com

First Avon Books printing: July 1996

Avon Trademark Reg. U.S. Pat. Off. and in Other Countries, Marca Registrada, Hecho en U.S.A.
HarperCollins® is a trademark of HarperCollins Publishers Inc.

Printed in the U.S.A.

10 9 8

For my son-in-law, Steve Harmon,
who loves both the mountains and the sea;
and for Alva Rex,
with whom I shared many an adventure and many
a book long ago when the two of us were young.

Special thanks to Larry Zimmerman—swordsman, genealogist, computer expert, and friend—who could have really done it, but didn't. Zemsa, Zim.

You think that you are . . . the pursuer . . . that it is your part . . . to prevail, to overcome. Fool: it is you who are the pursued, the marked-down quarry, the destined prey.

—G. B. Shaw
Man and Superman

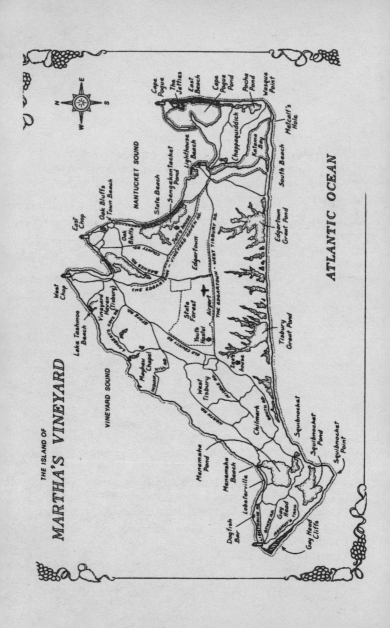

• 1 •

It all started with a bluefish blitz at Metcalf's Hole on South Beach. It was early summer and the bluefish were everywhere. After hitting the yard sales, Zee and I had taken a lunch out to Pocha Pond, on a beautiful, sunny Saturday morning. I had unfolded the old bedspread I use for a beach blanket, and while Zee lay on it in the lee of the tall rushes that grow there and read, I waded out for some chowder quahogs. For some reason, Pocha Pond doesn't seem to have any small quahogs, only big ones. How they make the jump from teeny seed to chowder size with no intervening steps is a mystery to me, although the Great Quahog God probably understands it perfectly. After I had my small basket full, I waded back to shore, and ogled Zee, who looked splendid in her wee bikini.

"Nice bod," I said.

Zee lifted her eyes. "By next month, you'll be a married man, so you're going to have to learn to stop drooling over single women."

"Next month is July. This is still June, and you're still single, so don't rush me."

"Come here," she said. "I want to explain something to you."

I went to her.

"Lean down."

I leaned down. She tossed her book, and pulled me down on top of her.

"Help, help," I whispered. "I'm being assaulted."

I was wet and cool, and she was warm and dry. Pretty soon we were both warm and wet.

"There," said Zee. "Let that be a lesson to you."

"I have short-term memory loss," I said, as we untangled and put our bathing suits back in place. "What was that we just did? Can we do it again?"

"I can do it again," said Zee, "but I think you'll need a few minutes before giving it another go. Meanwhile, let's eat."

We did that, washing lunch down with cold Sam Adams beer, and afterward we napped in the hot Martha's Vineyard sun, improving both our tans and our energies at the same time.

In mid-afternoon, Zee stretched and smiled. She looked like a long, lean cat. Her blue-black hair framed her tanned face, and her dark eyes were lazy and sensual. She leaned over me.

"Sorry," I said. "I'm saving myself for my marriage. I don't drool over single women anymore. I'm afraid I must ask you to be on your way."

She looked beyond me and sighed. "I'm afraid I must do just that. Here comes a caravan of Jeeps. Our haven is no longer ours alone."

I rolled over and looked. Sure enough, here came three trucks down from the Dike Bridge, headed for Wasque. Fishermen or picnickers coming back from Cape Pogue Pond, no doubt. I looked at my watch. Three o'clock. By the time we got home, it would be martini time. I gave Zee a chaste kiss, and we packed up.

But as we came off the Wasque reservation, what should we see but a line of ORV's at Metcalf's Hole.

"Hey," said Zee. "They're catching fish! Let's get over there!"

We did that, and found a gap where we could park my old Land Cruiser. Fishermen were shoulder to shoulder, and there were fish under every truck. We got our rods off the roof rack, and walked right down to the surf.

"There's at least two schools out there," said George Martin, hauling in a nice fish. "One outside and one in close. A lot of cut lines."

Zee made her cast and was instantly on. "Hot damn!" She set the hook and began working the fish. I made my cast and got a hit after about a half dozen turns on the reel. There were mega-fish out there.

"Blast and drat!" Zee's line was limp. "Cut off!" she said, reeling in as fast as she could.

I landed my fish just as she finished rerigging and headed back to the surf. She landed two fish before she was cut off again. She uttered a very unladylike word and headed back up to the truck.

I brought in my fifth fish as she was digging through her tackle box, looking for another leader. She found it and tied it on. "Don't say a thing," said Zee, looking up at me from under lowered brows. She ran down to the beach.

Five minutes later, she was back at the truck again, looking for yet another rig.

"I've told you to use a longer leader," I said helpfully, while I unhooked a nice eight-pounder right beside her. "Look at me. A thirty-inch leader, and I haven't been cut off once. But you and those eighteen-inchers. Why do you use those things? How many rigs have you lost this morning?"

"Shut up," explained Zee.

I cut my fish's throat and tossed it into the shade of the rusty Land Cruiser beside the others. Zee, rigged up once more, headed down to the surf to make her cast.

According to George Martin, the fish had come in just after noon and had been there ever since. They were taking anything you could throw out there, so all of us were using junk lures, and one thing worked as well as the next. It was terrific fishing, but a lot of gear was being lost to crossed lines and the fins and teeth of the voracious blues.

I probably have as much gear on the bottom of the

ocean as anyone else does, but today I'd been lucky. Not
a single lost lure. It was too good an opportunity to pass
up, so I didn't. I went down again and stood beside Zee
and made my cast. She was already on, her rod bent and
singing, and was bringing the fish in. There wasn't much
tide, so she didn't have to walk down the beach. Instead,
she was cranking him straight in.

"Now listen to old J. W.," I said, as I saw a swirl and
felt a fish take my lure. I set the hook and my rod bent.
"The secret of successful fishing is to keep the fish attached to the lure, and the lure attached to the leader,
and the leader attached to the line, and the line attached
to the reel, and the reel attached to the rod, and . . ."

"Shut up, Jefferson!" Her fish was giving her a lovely
fight.

"Be patient," I said, "there's more. . . . And the rod attached to you, the fisherperson. That's all there is to it.
Now you've got all of it right except the leader attached
to the line part, so that's the part you have to work on.
You should start by getting rid of all those eighteen-inch
leaders and make yourself some good long ones like I
use." I gave her my best smile.

"One more word, Jefferson, and the wedding's off!"

She landed her fish, gritted her teeth at me, and carried the fish up to the Land Cruiser. She was wearing
shorts and a tee shirt over her bathing suit, and had her
long, black hair tied up with a blue kerchief. She, like
me, had Tevas on her feet. On her left ring finger she
wore the small diamond that had been my grandmother's engagement ring. In four weeks, on July 13, we
planned to add a wedding ring to that finger.

I landed my fish. Another eight- or nine-pounder,
which was today's size. Schools of blues often are about
the same weight, for reasons probably known to Nep-
tune, but not to me. I carried it up to the truck.

Zee was counting fish. Hers were by the hind wheel
and mine were by the front wheel.

"I've got my limit," she said.

There is a ten-fish daily limit for sport fishermen. I

have a commercial license, so I can ignore it.

"You can catch some for me," I said.

"And have to listen to more of that long-leader stuff? Fat chance! Besides," she said, "I have to go to town and do some chores." She put her rod on the roof rack. "You can stay. I imagine that George will give me a ride home. Won't you, George?" She gave him her dazzling smile.

"Sure," said George, who was old enough to be her father, but was not blind.

"Never mind," I said. "I brought you out here, and since I'm a manly man with a code of ethics that requires self-sacrifice when women and children and dogs are in trouble, I'll take you home even though the fishing may never be this good again."

"Thanks anyhow, George," smiled Zee.

We drove west along the beach until we came to the pavement. There, where two-wheel-drive cars could park, the beach was still filled with the June People, getting their vacation money's worth as they squeezed the last advantage from the warm rays of the late afternoon sun. We turned right, crossed the Herring Creek, and went past the condominiums toward Edgartown. The bike path beside the road was full of bikers and walkers.

"What chores?" I asked.

"Well, for one thing, I have to get some more gear. I got cut off four times today, and I need some plugs and some new leaders. Don't say one word, Jefferson! But first I have to get some money because I don't have any."

"The banks are closed."

"Ah, but I have an ATM card and the Vineyard Haven National Bank has a machine right in Edgartown, so I am in business."

I did not have an Automatic Teller Machine card. Because my checkbook was never in balance anyway, I figured it would only get worse if I got an ATM card, since then I could get money without even having a check stub amount to improperly subtract from my current imbalance.

The traffic was pretty heavy, but then the Vineyard summer season was getting longer every year. At one time, the islanders had made almost all of their tourist money between July 4 and Labor Day, but nowadays the season stretched from May till October and even longer. A sure sign that summer had actually started was the number of mopeds on the road. Mopeds were a constant hazard to their drivers, many of whom knew nothing at all about how to stay on top of the little machines. The veteran island police officers preferred night duty to day duty simply because the moped accidents almost all took place in the daylight. So the younger the officer, the more likely it was that he or she would have the day shift, otherwise known as Moped Mop-up. Similarly, the hospital emergency room, where Zee often worked, was busy all summer repairing damaged moped riders or shipping the worst injured of them off to mainland hospitals on Cape Cod or up in Boston.

Mopeds held up traffic when they weren't doing worse things, and we followed a half dozen into town. As I loafed behind them down Pease Point Way, I suggested to Zee that maybe there should be an official moped season, with bounties available on a per-head basis. It was not an original idea.

"You don't have to knock off the mopeds," said Zee. "They self-destruct faster than Mr. Phelps's tapes."

True.

We turned up Main Street and drove into the A & P-Al's Package Store afternoon traffic jam. The citizens of Edgartown seem intent upon having as many traffic jams as they can manage, and from time to time rearrange the traffic patterns on the lovely, narrow streets of their village so as to maximize driving difficulties. They are very good at it, and have made it very difficult indeed to drive efficiently or park anywhere, but their crowning achievement is the traffic jam in front of the A & P and Al's Package Store. From time to time each day, all summer long, traffic is backed up a half mile or so in either direction, making Edgartown the undisputed winner of Worst-Traffic-Jam-on-the-Island champion-ship trophy.

Of course, as I often explained to Zee and anyone else who would (and some who wouldn't) listen, this jam, and most others, was caused by people making left turns. My plan was to put concrete barriers down the middle of the road in front of the A & P and Al's so no one could make any left turns.

"No left turns, no traffic jams. Put a traffic circle around Cannonball Park and another one around the Square Rigger, so people can reverse direction, and everything will be fine. But does anyone listen to me? No."

Zee rolled her eyes. "Yes, dear."

"Dear," I said. "I like that. It sounds like we're already married."

The Vineyard Haven National Bank's ATM booth was at the triangle, near the post office. I pulled into a park-ing place and Zee jumped out. While Zee dodged cars on her way to the ATM booth, I eyed the parking plan of the plaza, convinced once again that whoever had de-signed it had psychological problems. Cars were obliged to park or drive every which way, and everyone I'd ever talked to agreed that it was not only the worst parking design they'd ever seen, but that, since nobody could look in all the directions people were parking, walking, and driving, it was only a matter of time before some-body got run over trying to get to the P.O.

Zee made it to her ATM booth safely. I watched her enter with her magic card and punch buttons inside. She collected her money and looked at her receipt, then looked at it again. Then she looked at it some more. Then she put her card back into the machine and got another receipt. She looked at it. Then she put her money into her purse and came out of the booth.

"Guess what?" she said, climbing into the Land Cruiser.

"What?"

"You're looking at a wealthy woman." She smiled and waved her two receipts.

Nurses don't normally get wealthy so fast. "I want you to know," I said, "that it's your dear, sweet heart that has drawn me to you, and that your millions mean nothing to me."

"In that case," said Zee, "I'll just keep the hundred thousand to myself."

"A hundred thousand? Dollars?"

"Look," said Zee, handing me the receipts. "I have about fifteen hundred in my checking account, but look at these."

I looked. Each receipt said that Zee had a hundred thousand more than that in her account.

"I got two receipts, just to make sure," said Zee. "Both times it said the same thing. Maybe I should go right to the tackle shop and get myself a hundred thousand dollars' worth of leaders and lures. What do you think?"

"I think Rio might be a better plan, because I have a feeling that banks, being banks, probably have laws that protect them when this happens and put people like you in jail if you run off with the hundred thousand."

"Rio it is, then. They'll never catch us."

"We have to get rid of these fish before we go. And now that I think of it, I don't have a passport. You'll have to go alone, I'm afraid."

"Rats. Well, in that case, let's go get me some tackle instead."

"Remember. Long leaders this time. No more of those eighteen-inchers."

"I really hate it when people just can't let something go. You know what I mean?"

I did. We nosed into the traffic jam and stayed in it until we got to Chase Road, then cut up to Coop's, where Zee got herself two Roberts, two Missiles, and enough forty-five-pound test leader makings to keep her in business for a while.

"Tell you what," she said, as we left. "I'm going to give your friend Hazel Fine a call on Monday, and see what she says about this mistake in my account."

Hazel Fine worked at the Vineyard Haven National Bank. I had met her the year before. She was the only banker I knew very well, for I had lived a sheltered life.

"Good idea," I said. "Maybe we'll find out it isn't a mistake. Maybe we'll find out that you have a secret admirer who has decided to slip a hundred thou into your account every now and then in a vain hope of winning you away from me."

Zee grasped my arm and fluttered her lashes at me. "If you get his name, pass it on to me, and I'll make sure you get your grandma's ring back before the guy and I head for Cannes."

Zee's hundred thou was the first unusual thing that happened that week. It wasn't the last.

■ 2 ■

On Sunday morning Zee got a receipt from yet another ATM and still had her hundred thou. But by Monday morning it was gone. The Vineyard Haven National Bank informed her that she had just her fifteen hundred in her checking account.

"*Sic transit gloria mundi.*" She sighed, as she told me this over the phone. She was at work in the emergency room and had just called the bank and gotten the bad news.

"Did they give you any explanation?"

"They said they'd been having trouble with some of their machines."

"I told you you should have withdrawn the money while you had a chance."

"You did not. Oh well. No French Riviera again this year."

"Riviera schmiviera. You're already on the blessed isle of Martha's Vineyard. The Riviera holds no comparable charms. Besides, I'm here, not there. Think about that."

There was a silence at the far end of the line. I hummed into my phone. "I'm thinking, I'm thinking," she said, laughing. Then, "Oops, there's some business coming through the door. It has the appearance of the first moped spill of the day. Gotta run."

She hung up.

Another fortune slipped through our fingers. Oh well.

It was a lazy day, warm and sunny. I was wearing shorts and Tevas, my usual at-home garb during the summer. I put on my shades and went out to the garden and weeded and watered flowers and veggies for an hour. The lawn needed mowing, so I put in some more time doing that. By then it was time for the day's first beer, so I got a Sam Adams from the fridge and had that on my balcony, while I looked out toward the beach on the far side of Sengekontacket Pond, where the cars belonging to the June People were already lining the highway between Edgartown and Oak Bluffs.

The beach beyond the highway is a favorite one for young families, because the parking is free, the prevailing offshore wind and gently sloping shore create safe waters for small children, and the water is only a hundred feet or so from the road, making it easy for Mom and Dad to tote their armloads of gear and children from car to seashore.

On the beach, the bright umbrellas were up, and in the water beyond the sand the surf sailors were riding their multicolored sailboards back and forth across the gentle southwest wind. In the air, kaleidoscopic kites were flying. Although I could not see them, I knew the young mothers had their beach chairs facing the water so they could watch their children playing on the edge of the water. Their babies' cribs were beneath their umbrellas, their beachbags were stuffed with towels and toys, food and drink, sunscreen and lotions, diapers and books. Their husbands were flying the kites or reading or letting themselves be covered with sand by their children.

My Sam Adams was so good that I had another one, accompanied by some bluefish pâté, cheese, and crackers. Life was not bad. The sky was pale blue, and in the woods around the house the birds were talking. More birds were at the feeders I had hanging here and there. I wondered if they'd still come after Zee moved in and brought her cats, Oliver Underfoot and Velcro. I gave that some thought and decided that I could probably rig the feeders so Oliver and Velcro couldn't get at them. Of course the birds would have to watch out for themselves, cats being cats, but that was okay since both were God's little creatures. I wondered once again whether there were birds in cat heaven or cats in bird heaven. Once again, I really couldn't guess.

At eleven-thirty I phoned the Vineyard Haven National Bank and asked to speak with Hazel Fine.

Hazel's voice sounded musical as always.

"Let me take you to lunch," I said.

"Well, thank you, but I imagine that Mary has already fixed something at home."

"She can come, too."

"Why don't you join us instead?"

"I want to ask you some bank questions. Nothing serious, but if you eat my food, I won't feel guilty. If I eat yours . . ."

"I don't imagine you'll feel very guilty about that either, J. W. You're not the guilty type. Come by the house at twelve-thirty."

"I'll bring white wine."

"You and Mary can drink it. I'll have to go back to work."

"I think Mary and I can manage that."

She laughed. "I'll give Mary a ring so she'll be forewarned. See you in an hour."

Hazel Fine and Mary Coffin lived together in Vineyard Haven, a short walk from the bank and an even shorter one from the library. They were attractive women, both fortyish, who had been together for years. They were fond of early and baroque music, and were members of an island choral and orchestral group that I had hired to play at our wedding. Hazel had an excellent voice, and Mary played recorders, the oboe, and other wind instruments. They were also good cooks, so I made sure I arrived on time.

Mary was wearing a light green housedress and Hazel was in banker lady's clothes—blue suit and white blouse, low-heeled shoes, and some gold at her throat and wrist. I told them they both looked smashing, which was true as well as being politically correct.

Lunch was vichyssoise and thin ham and cucumber sandwiches. My bottle of vino verde was just right with it. Mary and I poured glasses for ourselves and iced water for Hazel, and we dug into the soup and sandwiches.

"Now what is this bank business you want to know about?" asked Hazel, touching her lips with a napkin.

I told her about Zee's hundred thousand dollars.

She smiled and shook her head. "We're installing a new computer system, and there are still some bugs in it. Our ATM's have their share of those bugs. I imagine that it was probably just a printing error in the machine."

"But Zee got the same information from another machine the next day. Could the same mistake occur in two different machines?"

"I wish I knew more about computers, but I imagine two machines can make the same mistake, just like two people can."

"I can make enough mistakes for two people all by myself," I said.

"I'll tell you what I'll do," said Hazel. "I'll look up Zeolinda's account myself, and check the balance."

"She called the bank this morning and the hundred thou was gone."

"I'm glad to hear that. All right, I'll double-check the balance and also check all transactions on her account for the last month. If there was an error during that time, we should catch it."

"If you find the hundred thousand and it doesn't belong to anybody, will you just slide it over into my account? I'll split it with you later."

"There are very few hundred thousands that don't belong to somebody, J. W." Hazel glanced at her watch. "I've got to get back. I'll call the bride-to-be at the hospital when I've checked her account."

She went out, and Mary and I finished the wine and sandwiches.

"Well," said Mary, "in a month you'll be a married man. How do you feel about that?"

"Fine. Anxious. Worried."

"Worried about what?"

"Worried that she'll change her mind. If she does, I'll have to start courting her all over again, and I may not be able to con her into this another time."

"I don't think you conned her, J. W." She smiled. "Relax. The wedding will be a great success and you'll live happily ever after. It's good when people find a partner to live with. I don't think we were meant to live alone."

"I've done more of it than I want to. How's the music shaping up?"

"It's well shaped."

We cleared the table and took the dishes into the kitchen. Then I found my hat—a baseball cap advertising CV 60, the USS *Saratoga*—and gave Mary a kiss on the cheek. "If Hazel can't get through to Zee at the hospital, have her give me a ring at home. I'll relay the message."

On my not-too-good truck radio, I got the classical music station in Chatham, and listened to the end of something by Bach on the way home. Bach often bores me, but this time he was okay. It's too bad he had so many children and so much work to do. If he'd had more time, maybe he could have spent it on each piece of music and would have written fewer that sound so much alike. When the station was through with Bach, they played a Beethoven piano concerto performed by David Greenstein, the latest winner of the Tchaikovsky competition in Moscow, and Zee's current musical passion. Better than Bach. Ludwig Van is the world's heavyweight music champion, and David Greenstein could really pound the ivories. He was still at it when I got home.

There, having had enough classical music, I switched to the C and W station that comes out of Rhode Island, and listened to Reba and Tanya and Garth and the other guys and gals sing their songs about love betrayed or gained. I like classical and C and W music, but you can have most of the other stuff, especially the current noise that kids listen to. Too hard on my ears, and too juvenile. C and W music may not be profound, but at least it's written for grown-ups.

I was fixing up a giant salad for supper when the phone rang. I thought maybe it would be Hazel, but it wasn't. It was Quinn.

"Coming down this weekend," said Quinn. "You got room?"

"I've got room."

"Bringing a guest."

"She's welcome."

"Not she, he."

"He's welcome. How long you staying?"

"Week?"

"Sounds good."

"How are the fish running?"

"So many they're standing on their tails so they'll all fit in the ocean."

"Dynamite! See you Friday night. We're bringing the pizzas and beer. Tell that sweetheart of yours to cheer up because a real man is on his way!"

"I'll try to keep her calm."

Quinn hung up.

Quinn was a reporter for the *Globe*. I had met him when I was a cop for the Boston P.D. and we had hit it off. After I'd taken the bullet that still nestled next to my spine, and had retired to the Vineyard in search of a more peaceful career, Quinn and I had kept in touch, the touch being mostly in the form of my going up to Boston once a year to catch the Sox in Fenway and have a few beers at the Commonwealth Brewery, makers of America's best bitter, and Quinn's coming to the island to have a go at the wily bluefish. Next to nailing a good story, Quinn liked nothing better than nailing the blues.

It would be good to see Quinn, and I looked forward to having him down a couple weeks before the wedding. He would loosen things up in case they got tight. Quinn didn't let things get tight. He disapproved of tight, except for occasionally being that way by dint of booze.

I wondered who his friend was. Since his divorce, Quinn had taken up with a number of women, but had never remarried. Once or twice, he had brought women down to the island with him, and I had put them up in my spare bedroom, which is normally only occupied by my father's hand-carved decoys. There were twin beds in there, so this time Quinn and his friend would also have that room. Someday, maybe, it would be a child's room. But not yet.

A half hour after Quinn had called, the phone rang again. I was making some pesto bread to go with the salad, and having a Sam Adams. This time it was Hazel Fine.

"I called the hospital, but Zeolinda was busy with someone who had just come into the emergency room."

"She'll be here for supper, if you want to talk with her personally."

"Oh no. You can pass the word, such as it is. Tell her that I checked her account from April till now, and there's no sign of any hundred thousand dollars or any other error. I think we can blame it on a couple of faulty ATM machines. A computer glitch of some kind."

"A hundred-thousand-dollar glitch is a pretty good glitch."

"Yes it is. As I told you, we're installing a new computer system here at the bank. Until now, we've had a servicer over on the mainland doing all of our computer work, but that got too expensive, so we've decided to do all of our processing in-house. We've had problems transferring the accounts from there to here, and this balance error is apparently just another one of them. It probably happened late last week, and didn't get corrected until this morning."

"I thought you bankers didn't make mistakes."

"You thought that, eh? Say, I have a deal in real estate—a bridge in New York—that might interest you."

We laughed. I'm so bad at handling my own money that I'm probably qualified to open a savings and loan of my own.

When Zee came in, tired after a long day of putting people back together after sundry mishaps, I sent her right to the shower. After she came out, feeling better, I gave her a martini and took her up to the balcony. There, I plied her with hors d'oeuvres and more martinis while I gave her Hazel's message and told her of Quinn.

She liked Quinn. "It'll be good to see him again. Who's his friend?"

"I didn't catch his name."

The news of the coming of Quinn and his companion was the second thing that happened that week. The third thing happened on Wednesday. It was a very bad thing.

■ 3 ■

Martha's Vineyard draws young people like honey draws bees. They swarm down from the mainland every spring and take up jobs that pay peanuts for the sake of spending a summer in the island sun. They promise to work faithfully until Labor Day, but quit in mid-August, as their employers know they will, so they can have a couple of weeks of uninterrupted fun before returning to college. If they break even over the summer, they are happy. They are usually happy anyway, since it's hard to be unhappy when you're twenty years old and sun, sex, surf, and beer are in such plentiful supply.

Only young people from abroad, the Irish and the like, keep working into the fall, since the money they make on the island, however meager, is more than they can make at home.

These summer citizens live in shacks in the woods, or group illegally in large houses in violation of town ordinances which are ignored by their slumlords. The slumlords can make a pretty penny from their summer guests, and care little at all about the condition of their buildings or their occupants, or about the opinions of their neighbors.

Just after I pulled out of my driveway late Wednesday afternoon and headed for Edgartown, I met one of the youthful summer persons coming along the other side of the road on a wobbly moped. Bound home after a day's work, I guessed. She had long brown hair and would have been quite pretty if the expression on her face had not been so strained. Was she thinking bad thoughts about her boss or boyfriend, or just trying to stay on top of her restless moped? I thought she should try to look less severe, so her frown lines wouldn't become habitual, and recalled my father warning me that if I kept sucking my thumb I'd grow up looking like Eleanor Roosevelt.

I had spent the afternoon refiberglassing the bottom of my dinghy. I had worn a hole in its bottom by dragging it over the sand when I launched or retrieved it from Collins Beach, where I kept it log-chained to the bulkhead during the summer. It was now in the back of the Land Cruiser, and I was returning it to the log chain which prevented Edgartown's gentlemen summer sailors from stealing it so they could get back out to their yachts late at night after the launch service had ended. I drove down Cooke Street, fetched the Reading Room dock, and made the dinghy fast. Inside the Reading Room, the men were having cocktails. Only men had cocktails at the Reading Room, I'd been told, except for a couple of hours on Sunday nights, when wives and ladies-in-waiting were allowed to share the booze.

I had not been invited to the cocktail hour, so I parked the Land Cruiser on the beach, and walked down South Water Street, past the giant Pagoda Tree and various inns and hotels, to Main Street. There I took a right and popped in at the Wharf pub, where at that time I could get a glass of Commonwealth Brewery Ale, America's finest beer. The pub was full of young people and noise, but the beer made the stop worthwhile, so I had not one but two before returning to the street.

There I met the chief of the Edgartown police, looking fairly composed for a man whose Vineyard summer had already started. The chief was watching one of his summer rent-a-cops trying to handle the mix of cars and pedestrians at the four corners, where Water Street and Main Street intersect. The rent-a-cop was not doing too badly, and the chief saw no need to interfere, even though the walkers were, as usual, crossing the street without looking or slowing down. Happily for the rent-a-cop, the drivers were both slow and alert, so no bumps or bruises had yet occurred, and the rent-a-cop was able to keep both vehicles and people on the move.

The chief and I walked away from the intersection and down to the parking lot in front of the yacht club. Out in the harbor, a few yachts were swinging at their moorings. There would be a lot more later. On a stake between the yacht club and the Reading Room my cat-boat, the *Shirley J.*, pointed her nose into the falling southwest wind.

"Did you see that crowd?" said the chief. "It looks like the Fourth of July and here it is only June. More cars and people every year!"

"That's what you said last year."

"I think this may be my last year. I can't take this anymore. I think I'll retire and rent a place up in Nova Scotia for the summer. They say that up there it's like it used to be here twenty years ago."

"That's what you said last year."

"I'll come back down here after Labor Day. It's not so bad then."

"That's what you said last year."

"I know I said it last year, but this time I really mean it. The other day when I came out of the station, this woman stops her car and asks me, 'Is this the right road?' That's all. Just, 'Is this the right road?' Not 'Is this the right road to Katama?' or 'Is this the right road to the airport?' Just, 'Is this the right road?' Ye gods, what kind of a question is that? Then, about an hour later I was up in front of the A & P and damned if a guy doesn't stop his car and ask me the very same thing. That's when I knew it was time to go up to Nova Scotia."

"What did you tell those people?"

"I did the right thing. I smiled and said yes, it was. And they drove off."

"Clever. And some people think you're simple-minded."

"Speaking of simple minds, are you still planning to marry Zee now that she's just a poor working girl without a hundred thousand in her account?"

"How'd you find out about that?"

"I ran into your betrothed and she told me about her rapid rise to riches and her equally rapid return to normalcy. Too bad. You two could have afforded a humdinger of a honeymoon. Where you going, by the way?"

"I thought we might go to your house. Annie could cook for us and you could open the champagne and run errands. What do you think?"

"It's all right with me if you move in. I expect to be in Nova Scotia."

"In that case, I'll have to change my plans. We'll need somebody to serve us breakfast in bed, and shine our shoes, and stuff like that."

"Actually, this island is a good place to have a honeymoon. A lot of people spend an awful lot of money to do it. Annie and I did it ourselves. Of course that was because we were too poor to leave."

"It's not too bad being so poor that you have to live on Martha's Vineyard. I can imagine being poor in a lot of worse places."

"You don't know what poor is. You've got government money pouring in every month."

Not pouring, really, but at least dribbling. A bit from the Boston P.D. for carrying the bullet next to my spine, and some benefits from the USA as compensation for some Vietnamese shrapnel, bits of which still oozed out of my legs now and then. Any hopes I might have had of making a career as a male model had been done in, thanks to the scars bestowed upon me by people trying to kill me. I had collected some more scars since coming down to the Vineyard for good, but I didn't get any money for those.

"Your favorite reporter is arriving this weekend," I said. "Quinn. He's bringing a friend."

"Quinn!" The chief spat out the name. Some time before, Quinn had covered a drug bust on the island and had produced a story that was unflattering to the DEA and the various police agencies which had let the big guys get away while rounding up the small fry.

"I'm taking him and his friend fishing. You want to come along?"

"I don't have time to fish. I have to work for a living. Besides, Quinn and I don't hit it off too well."

"You barely know each other. It would be a good change for you to pursue the wily bluefish instead of the local perps."

"Quinn's a perp as far as I'm concerned."

"You're getting an awfully thin skin in your declining years."

The chief climbed into the cruiser that was parked across from the coffee shop.

"It's not a thin skin. It's a Quinn skin," he said. "I've got a thin skin for Quinn. Nobody else."

"Quinn just doesn't trust people in authority. That's why he's a good reporter."

"Hell, I don't trust them, myself. But then, I don't trust reporters either."

"In that case, it sure makes me proud to know that you trust me."

"Stand back from the window," said the chief. "I think I'm going to be sick."

I stood back and the chief backed out of his parking place, arched a brow, and drove away.

I walked over to the dock and watched the local fishing boats come in to unload their customers. From the looks of their catches, they were nailing the blues offshore. I went fishing offshore in the *Shirley J.* sometimes, but when I did it was a long day, since catboats are not famous for their speed. As far as I knew, I was the only offshore fisherman who still used a sailboat. I didn't think the idea would catch on among the commercial guys.

I walked back up past the Navigator Room, the restaurant with Edgartown's best harbor view and some of its best food, hooked a left on South Water Street, and went back to Collins Beach.

The cocktails were still flowing at the Reading Room, but I still hadn't gotten my invitation to join in, so I climbed into the old Land Cruiser and headed home.

The narrow streets of Edgartown were already mid-season busy. The white houses, and the gray-shingled houses, and the green lawns and bright flowers were elegant as always. The June People were on the sidewalks, happy to be in so lovely a place on such a fine, soft, summer evening.

The A & P traffic jam was in full bloom, but I was in a good mood and survived it with barely a curse. I popped out on its far side and was pleased to see a long line, which I was not in, backed up in the opposite direction. It's nice to not be in someone else's line.

I stopped at the head of my long, sandy driveway and got my mail, then drove on down toward my house. About two thirds of the way down, I saw the moped lying in front of me. I stopped and got out. Beyond the moped, there were footprints in the sand of the driveway. I followed them. They wandered down toward my house. After a hundred yards, the footprints veered off into the trees. I found the girl there. She had long brown hair, and I recognized her as being the moped rider I'd seen earlier on the highway. She smelled of vomit and diarrhea, and there were flecks of foam at her mouth. I could find no pulse at her neck or wrist. Her eyes were wide and staring. I left her there and jogged down to the house and called 911.

Finding the girl was the very bad thing that happened.

■ 4 ■

I was back at the Land Cruiser when the first wailing patrol car arrived from Edgartown. Behind it was an ambulance with its flashing lights.

Tony D'Agostine got out of the cruiser. "Can you move your truck?"

"The girl's about a hundred yards farther on," I said. "I may be wrong, but I don't think there's any rush. I thought you'd want a look at this moped and the girl's tracks before I changed anything."

"Okay," said Tony. He looked over his shoulder at the medics getting out of the ambulance. "Bring your gear," he called. "The victim's down ahead."

"You might want to tell them to go down the side of the driveway so they don't mess up the girl's tracks any more than I already have."

"Go down the side of the driveway so you don't mess up the girl's tracks," said Tony, as the first medics came by. "What about the tracks?" he said to me.

"They wander around. Like the girl was staggering."

"Hurt when the moped fell over?"

"I don't think she was staggering because she was hurt. I think she was sick." I told him about seeing her on the highway and about the smells and froth I'd noticed when I found her.

More police cars arrived, stacking up behind the ambulance. Policemen came walking down the driveway.

24

One of them had a camera. After he took pictures of the moped, several of us walked down the driveway looking at the girl's tracks. When we got to the girl, a medic looked up and shook his head. He and the other medics kept working on her anyway. I was glad I didn't have their job. The policeman with the camera took some more pictures. A medic got up.

"We aren't going to get her back." He looked at me. "You the guy who found her?"

"Yes. This is my driveway."

"Do you know her?"

"No."

"Then what was she doing down your driveway?"

I didn't like his tone. "Dying," I said.

He gave me a sour look. Tony D'Agostine took my arm. "Come on," he said. "Let's move that moped out of the way and then get your truck and some of these other vehicles on down to your house so we can get rid of this traffic jam."

When we got back to the moped, we took a look at it. It seemed all right to me. We pushed it off to one side of the driveway, and I led the caravan of cars down to my yard. There, most of the police cars turned around and went back to town, and the ambulance turned around and went back to the body.

Tony got out his notebook and took down the little I could tell him, then we walked back up to the body.

"We're ready to take her in," said the medic.

"What do you think, Miles?" asked Tony.

"Vomit, diarrhea, foam at the mouth. Something toxic. I imagine they'll find the agent in her stomach, whatever it was," said the medic. He looked at the body on the canvas. "Jesus, she was a pretty girl. What a way to go." He looked at me. "Looks to me like she drove down here trying to get help. Too bad nobody was home. Or were you?"

He was a big guy and he looked tired and angry.

"I'm sorry I wasn't," I said.

"Why'd she come looking for you?" he asked. "Why

did she think you'd be the one to help her?"

"I think it was just the first driveway she came to," I said, carefully. I realized that my right hand had become a fist, and I opened it into a hand again.

Miles turned to Tony D'Agostine. "We found this stuff in her pockets." He handed Tony a driver's license, a college ID, and some mail. "Name's Katherine Ellis. Lived in New Jersey. College kid. NYU." He gave me a last look, then bent to the stretcher. "Okay, let's go." He and the other medics picked Katherine Ellis up and put her in the ambulance and drove away.

"Miles is not a bad guy," said Tony D'Agostine. "It's just that he's got a daughter not much older, and she's hanging around with a guy he doesn't like. I think he just transferred all that to you."

Transferred. Everybody's a psychologist. "It's okay," I said.

Tony leafed through Katherine's mail. "Looks like she just came from the post office. Letter, postcard. Now I've got to find out where she's been living, then contact her folks and give them the news. People think cops chase bad guys all the time, but this is what we really do. I hate this part of it. Enough to make you hang up the tin."

"I'm surprised you're on duty. I thought you old pros were careful not to work the day shift."

"I'm herding our summer people till they get the hang of things." He looked around one more time. "Well, I'd better get going. I have to make some phone calls."

We walked down to my house. "I'll have that moped picked up," he said, and he drove away.

Across Sengekontacket Pond there were still a few cars parked beside the road. Their owners were salvaging the last of the evening sun, unaware that a half mile away a young woman had died miserably beside my driveway.

I felt invaded, somehow. Young women didn't die beside my driveway. I knew they died somewhere, but they did it someplace else. They fell off their mopeds on the highways or drove their cars into faraway trees or lost themselves in the city. But they didn't die two hundred feet from my house.

I went inside and fixed myself a vodka on the rocks. I put my tape of Carreras, Domingo, and Pavarotti into my machine and listened to Carreras sing "Federico's Lament." I don't understand Italian, but the lament sounded like what I was feeling. Then the other voices sang and after a while my self-pity was carried away and buried in that place where music sets us free.

That evening I phoned Zee and told her about Katherine Ellis. A half hour later her little Jeep pulled into my yard, and she stepped out, carrying an overnight case. It felt good to see her.

The next day, after Zee went to work, a pickup came down my driveway. It stopped in my yard where it could turn around. I was weeding in the garden. I went out to meet it. There was a young couple in the cab. The woman looked about Katherine Ellis's age and was red-eyed. The man was a year or two older. His face was strained, and he seemed ill at ease, as people often are in the aftermath of death.

"You must be Mr. Jackson," said the woman, rolling down her window. "The police told me your name. I'm Beth Goodwin. I'm . . . was Kathy's roommate. This is Peter Dennison. He's . . . a friend."

"Kathy's friend, too," said Peter Dennison. He reached a thin arm across in front of the woman and shook my hand. He looked tall and lanky, and wore wire-rimmed glasses. "We came to get the moped. It belonged to Kathy. We'll have to see what her family wants to do with it." His eyes floated past me. "Nice garden."

"The police have the moped," I said.

My voice went right past Beth Goodwin. "Peter has a garden, too," she said, in that awkward way that people have when they don't know what they should be saying.

"I'm sorry about your friend," I said. "Do they know yet what happened?"

"No," she said. "I just can't imagine! She was never

sick. Then to have this happen. It's awful to have to tell
people. We had to tell the Katama Caterers. That's where
she worked, you know. And think of her parents, and
poor Gordy, and the others. How they must feel . . ."

Peter Dennison shook his head. "She was the healthiest person I knew."

"I imagine they'll do tests," said the woman vaguely,
her voice trailing off.

Peter Dennison took a deep breath. "If the police already have the moped, we'd better get going," he said
apologetically.

I stepped back. "I am sorry about your friend," I said
again. "And, yes, they will do tests, but I don't know if
they'll do them here or on the mainland, so it may take
some time before they know the results."

"I've told the police that I want to know," said Beth
Goodwin.

"I'm sure they'll tell you."

The pickup drove away. It had New Jersey plates, and
there was an NYU sticker on the rear window. It looked
as if the three of them had come up from school together
to work on the island for the summer. But as someone
said, life is what happens when you plan something else.

Life is also what keeps going on for the rest of us after
it's stopped for the Katherine Ellises, so I went back and
finished my morning's work in the garden. I had flowers
along the front and back fences, next to the house, and
in hanging pots suspended from tree limbs beside some
of the bird feeders. My veggies were in raised beds inside of old railroad ties that I'd had hauled down from
America. A long time back, the Vineyard had its own
railroad, but those ties had rotted long ago. The Depot
gas station in Edgartown is a memory of the old railroad
line, and occasionally people still come across rusty railroad spikes.

I had a lot of fledgling weeds that were planning to
seize control of my flowers and veggies. If you could
find a commercial use for weeds, you could make a fortune. They grow when you want to grow other things

and they grow when you don't want to grow other things. When you fertilize your veggies and flowers, you fertilize your weeds, too. There is a moral in this weed lore, but I wasn't sure I wanted to know what it was. I weeded until my weeding capacity was all used up, then had a beer.

It was a beautiful day. Katherine Ellis would have loved it. I pushed her away from me. If I had never heard of her, or if I'd only read about her death, she'd be just as dead, but I wouldn't feel this way. It was because I'd seen her and because she'd died on my land that she was on my mind.

I put together a sandwich and washed it down with another beer while I listened to a tape of Ricky Scaggs singing about troubles with women. Ricky sang well, but he seemed to have even more problems than I did, so he didn't cheer me up too much. When Ricky was done and the sandwich was gone, I was wishing that Zee was with me. But she wasn't, and I had company coming, so I got my small basket and rubber gloves and went clamming.

Normally, I like clamming whether I'm with company or alone. With company, I can clam and talk at the same time; alone, I can clam and think about whatever's interesting. About Zee, for instance. Now, there was a good subject, one that would keep me from brooding about Katherine Ellis. I let my thoughts of Zee take over my mind while I drove to Eel Pond.

You can dig for clams with your hands, or with a shovel or a clam digger, or with a toilet plunger on the end of a stick, or probably in a dozen other ways I don't know about. Everybody has his favorite technique. Mine is to get down on my hands and knees and find the little devils by touch. I can get them that way about as fast as any other way, and I break fewer shells.

For a while I found no clams, but I was patient, and in time I began to work my way into the clamming fields. I hummed, "Oh, My Darling Clamming Time," the clammer's song, and wondered who Quinn's guest was. Whoever he was, Quinn would want to introduce him to the joys of Vineyard living, which included catching and eating lots of bluefish, clams, and quahogs. I figured that tomorrow night we could start this education with a clam boil to welcome the boys to the island, then on Saturday night we'd probably have a big bluefish blowout. It sounded like a good plan to me. I hoped that Quinn would bring plenty of beer. The pizza he'd promised could wait, or maybe serve as lunch. It was nice to think about food.

I worked until I had enough clams for four people and a few more, then waded back across the water and walked to the truck. I got a five-gallon pail and filled it full of saltwater, put a lid on it so the water wouldn't spill, and drove home. There, inside my outdoor shower, where the sun couldn't get to it, I put the five-gallon pail down and dumped the clams into it. The clams would spit out the sand in their systems overnight, and by the time Quinn and his friend arrived would be clean and ready to eat.

I phoned Zee at the hospital and invited her to tomorrow's clam boil. She said yes. Then I got my quahog rake and the same clam basket I'd just emptied, and drove to the south end of Katama Bay, where I usually found littlenecks and cherrystones. I raked for a while until I began to come up with keepers instead of the small seed quahogs that were so thick there. Once I found the keepers, I did pretty well, and in an hour had all that I needed.

I thought about going on over to Pocha to get some stuffers, but decided instead to use the ones I already had in my freezer. They would be good enough for the likes of me and my guests.

The next day I thawed my frozen quahogs and made stuffers—ground cooked quahog meat, onion, garlic, linguiça, bread crumbs, and some hot pepper all mixed together, topped with a bit of bacon and put back in large half shells to be baked until hot. Then I opened my cherrystones and made a few dozen clams casino. Even people who say they don't like clams like clams casino. I use Euell's recipe, which is as good as any. Finally, I opened the littlenecks and put them in the fridge to get cold with the other stuff.

The clams out of the way, I washed off potatoes, peeled the top layer off some onions, and cut more lin-guiça into two-inch hunks. I got out my big stainless steel pot and my trusty gas grill. I had salvaged the grill from the Edgartown dump in the golden days of yester-year, before the environmentalists seized control of it and ruined the priceless free recycling tradition that had once made a trip to the dump both an adventure and possibly a financial bonanza. In the old days, the dump was The Big D, the island's best department store, with 100 percent guaranteed return policy if you weren't com-pletely satisfied with your purchase. Now it was just the dump.

Zee drove in after work, gave me a kiss, took a quick shower, and climbed into shorts and a shirt whose tails she tied around her flat belly. She accepted the martini I gave her. I informed her that she looked smashing, which she did.

Since we had some time before Quinn was due, we went up onto the balcony, accompanied by some crack-ers and cheese and a pitcher of martinis.

Experience had shown that the two of us couldn't hold hands as long as there was food and drink available, so we didn't even try that. We looked across the pond and she told me about her day. We were still up there when Quinn's car came down the driveway.

Quinn pulled into the yard, stopped, and got out. Conscious of the seedy reputation a lot of reporters have, he always dressed well. He was still wearing his tie, in fact, which probably could have allowed him to pass as a lawyer down at the Dukes County Courthouse, since on Martha's Vineyard only Lawyers wear ties in the summertime.

He raised a hand. "Hail!"

The passenger door opened and a man about Zee's

age got out. He was wearing a white shirt open at the neck, dark summer trousers, and sandals. He was dark-haired and good-looking. He smiled up at us and lifted a hand.

Quinn gestured with his raised hand. "Dave, the tall one is J. W., your host. The pretty one who, as you can see, is already panting at the thought of my spending a few days here, is Zee, who has the foolish idea that she's going to marry him instead of me. J. W. and Zee, this is my friend Dave."

"Hi," said Dave.

"Oh, my God," whispered Zee, clutching my arm with one hand and waving with the other. "Do you know who that is?"

"No," I said. "Should I?" I lifted my free arm. "Hey, Dave. Welcome to the Vineyard."

"That's David Greenstein!" whispered Zee. "David Greenstein, the pianist! Holy smoke!"

I hadn't seen her so excited since she'd landed her forty-two-pound bass.

■ 5 ■

David Greenstein didn't look like the world's champion pianist. He was about five ten, one fifty, slim and athletic-looking. He had brown eyes and short dark hair. His nails were short and clean, and his hands were pretty ordinary. He could have been an accountant, maybe, or a lawyer, or a schoolteacher. Some kind of white-collar guy. A classical pianist? I wouldn't have guessed it, but then I have no idea what a classical pianist is supposed to look like. I guess I thought they always had long hair. On the other hand, logic suggested that, like people in other professions, classical pianists probably came in various sizes and shapes.

But what did I know?

Zee was first off the balcony. She kissed Quinn and shook David Greenstein's hand. She was very excited. When I was finished with my own handshaking, we hauled the suitcases into the spare bedroom.

"It's very good of you to have us, Mr. Jackson," said David Greenstein with a smile. For the first time I detected a weariness in him.

"Call me J. W.," I said. "Glad you could make it."

"Of course you and Dave will bunk here," said Quinn to me, putting his arm around Zee. "Zee and I will take the other room."

Zee smiled up at him. "You've been chasing women

ever since your pet sheep died. You've got to get another one."

"You can't embarrass me," said Quinn. "Dave knows exactly what kind of guy I am. He and I have known each other since he was knee high."

"You mean he knows everything?" asked Zee. She looked at David Greenstein. "It must be hard for you to keep from going to the police."

"Nonsense," said Quinn. "And I've told him all about you, too. How you only took up with J. W. because I was so far away. How you write me all those steamy letters. How you can barely keep from tearing off my clothes as soon as I get here. He knows all about you."

"You're a hell of a guy, Quinn," said Zee. "But look over there. You're embarrassing Jefferson."

Quinn withdrew his arm and made little patting gestures in the air with his hand. "Oh, all right. Yes, I suppose appearances must be maintained. At least for tonight. Okay, I'll bunk here with Dave. J. W. is so conventional."

"Stuffy is as stuffy do," I said, and we walked back out into the living room. Quinn fell into a chair.

"Dave and I both need a rest," he said. "We've been working too hard."

"Dave may have been working hard," I said, "but you?"

"The pursuit and publication of the truth are exhausting," said Quinn. "Only those of us who are blessed with extraordinary vitality and integrity, to say nothing of literary genius, can maintain the pace demanded of the fourth estate. And even we need to take a bluefishing break now and then."

"Well, the fish are in," said Zee, looking at David Greenstein. "Do you fish, David?"

"We used to fish for trout up in New Hampshire. But I've never fished in the ocean."

"Tomorrow you'll get your chance."

"I'm looking forward to it."

"You know where the booze is," I said to Quinn. "It's

every man for himself, I'm going to get the grill fired up."

"Grill?" asked Quinn.

"Grill as in steamed clams."

Quinn got up. "Hot damn! I'll go get the beer out of the trunk, then I'll give you a hand."

"I'll show you where we hide the vodka," said Zee to David Greenstein. "Then you and I can go up on the balcony and loaf while these two guys slave for us. I want you to see how well I've got Jefferson trained."

"I hope you're not allergic to clams, because you're getting several versions of them," I said to Dave an hour later, as I placed the first course—littlenecks on the half shell—on the table out on the lawn. Then I had a sudden thought. "Or maybe you just plain don't eat shellfish."

Dave laughed. "I eat anything. Cast-iron stomach. We never had a kosher house. I've had these before." He put some seafood sauce on his first littleneck and slid it into his mouth. The rest of us followed suit.

The littlenecks were cold and delicious. We had white wine and beer to help wash them down. When the littlenecks were gone, I broiled the casinos and we ate those while the stuffers baked and the steamers steamed. Then we ate the stuffers. Then I took the potatoes, onions, and chunks of linguiça out of the steamer and put them into bowls, and served them up with the steamed clams.

By the time we were through, it was dark, and we were all bulging at the seams.

"Not bad," said Zee, loosening the top button of her shorts. "I do believe that you have a career as a clam boil chef ahead of you, should you choose to accept the assignment, Mr. Phelps."

We dumped the paper plates and shells into a trash barrel and I brought out the coffee and cognac. Above us the Milky Way arced across a starry sky. The lights of some plane headed for Europe moved slowly from west to east among the stars, and the wind sighed softly through the trees. An owl hooted in the distance.

David Greenstein leaned back in his chair and smiled. "This is the way to live. I can see why you stay down here." He yawned. "Sorry."

"It's the Island Sleepies," said Zee. "When people first get to the Vineyard, they get overwhelmed by the Island Sleepies. I don't know whether it's the salt air, or what, but you get so sleepy you can't stay awake. It even happens to me when I've been away for a while. The cure is to give in and go to bed. No apologies required."

"Thanks," he said. "It sounds wonderful. I'll do it." He got up. "Great meal. Good night, all."

He walked into the house. Zee looked after him for a moment.

"He's nice," she said.

"Yeah," said Quinn. "He's been working very hard. Too hard."

"He won't have to work here," I said. "No piano."

Quinn looked at me. "Ah, you know who he is."

"Zee knew. She's a fan."

"He's a wonderful player," said Zee. "And he's so young."

"He's twenty-eight," said Quinn. "We both grew up in Evanston. I met him when he was just a kid. We lived next door. I was a sort of big brother. We used to sneak off to White Sox or Cubs games sometimes when he should have been home practicing. His mother did not love me for that, but his dad understood. Later he and his dad and I used to go up-country trout fishing. Dave and I played hoops together at the gym, and went to a movie now and then. Stuff like that. Then we grew up and I got married and then divorced and he got famous and we both moved. I went to Boston and he's been around the world a dozen times."

"Then he won the Tchaikovsky competition," said Zee. "I have a record of him playing Liszt. Incredible!"

"He's got a manager who keeps him on the run. Too much. Dave looks good, but he needs a rest." Quinn sipped his cognac. "He called me from New York last week. Said he needed to get away. I thought of this place." He glanced at us. "A few days where nobody knows who he is or what he does." He grinned his wry Irish grin. "I've stolen him away, you might say. He was supposed to play at Symphony Hall tonight and for the next two nights and then go on to St. Louis. But he's not going to be there, and so there will be a stink raised. Worse yet, even his manager won't know where he is. It will be quite a story. You should see it in tomorrow's papers."

Zee frowned. "Won't this get him into trouble? Won't people sue him for breaking his contracts?"

"Maybe. Maybe not. Dave left his manager a note telling him not to worry, but to tell everybody that he was sick, and that the doctors say he'll be back on the tour in a week. He didn't say where he was going, or that he was going with me."

I looked at him. "Will any of your buddies at the *Globe* figure it out? They know you like to come down here, and they must know that you two know each other. If I was a reporter and I knew that, and if you and David Greenstein just happened to disappear at the same time, I know where I'd start to look. Too good a story not to."

"Yeah, except I told everybody I was going to Chicago to visit my sister and catch some Cubs games."

"You have a sister in Chicago?"

"Yeah, and she'll lie for me, too. Anybody contacts her and asks if I'm there, she'll say yes. She's a good kid. Loves her big brother. Do anything for him. I told her that if anybody asks her if Dave is out there, she's to hedge, then hint that he is. She said it was no problem as long as Dave gives her two tickets for his next Chicago concert. Her husband is a classical piano freak."

I shook my head. "You're a sweetheart of a guy, Quinn."

"You hear that, Zee? I've been telling you that for years, and now J. W.'s finally admitting it. You belong with me, kid."

"You're too good for me, I'm afraid," said Zee, taking my arm. "I like the low-life type."

"You guys will keep quiet about Dave?"

"I don't know about Zee," I said, "but I plan on selling the story to the *National Tattler* as soon as I can find their telephone number."

"Tell him not to shave," said Zee. "A lot of guys do that when they're down here on vacation. He'll look like everybody else."

"If he hangs around us, he'll be fine," I said. "We go places and do things that don't interest the gossip columnists."

"A week of fishing and quahogging is just what he needs." Quinn nodded. "No piano, no photographs, no audience."

"I think we can manage that. It's a perfect description of the way we live." I looked at Zee. "We can make him your cousin Dave from New Bedford. What do you think?"

"Sounds good. He'll be the first cousin I ever had who won the Tchaikovsky competition."

"I guess I wouldn't mention that part to anyone," said Quinn. He poured himself a bit more cognac. "Well, now that that's settled, when do we go after the blues?"

"If I thought you two would get out of bed, we could leave at four tomorrow morning. But I doubt if Dave will be ready to roll out of the sack by then, so why don't both of you sleep in, and we'll get out to Wasque about ten. The fish have been around all day, sometimes, so we may have a shot at them, even though we won't get there early. I thought maybe I'd bake up a couple tomorrow night."

"An excellent plan."

"Of course, you have to catch 'em before I can cook 'em."

"No problem." Quinn yawned.

"I think the Sleepies have got you, too," said Zee.

Quinn finished his drink and climbed to his feet. "Right you are. Until the morrow, then." He looked at the trees. "The night above the dingle starry," he said, and walked into the house.

After a while, Zee said, "David Greenstein right here in your house. Imagine that!"

"I'm here too," I said.

"Yes, but you don't play the piano."

"I play the guitar."

"You play it with your thumb."

"Of course I play it with my thumb. That's the way you play a guitar. You thumb it."

"David Greenstein won the Tchaikovsky competition."

"He won the Tchaikovsky piano competition. I won the Tchaikovsky guitar-thumbing competition, but I just never got around to telling you before."

"You are the soul of modesty, Jefferson. It's one of the characteristics that makes you so lovable."

"How true, how true."

Across the pond we could see the lights of cars moving between Edgartown and Oak Bluffs. Beyond them, off to the right, was the flash of the Cape Pogue lighthouse, and on the far side of Nantucket Sound the lights on Cape Cod glimmered. Arched above them all were the bright stars and the silver Milky Way. It was a warm and starry, starry night.

"Let's go to bed," said Zee, suddenly, taking my hand.

"Okay."

I started to pick things up to take them into the house, but Zee said, "No. Leave everything. We'll get it in the morning. I want you to come and hug me. And I want to hug you. Come on."

I thought that she had been thinking about David Greenstein.

She took my hand and led me into the house.

■ 6 ■

The only trouble with fishing on Saturday in the summertime is that all the people who work during the week fish on Saturday. The Jeeps start piling up at Wasque before sunrise, and they keep coming until afternoon. Fishermen wander in their four-by-fours from site to site, looking for blues. They cast their lines at all the Chappy fishing spots—Metcalf's Hole, Wasque, East Beach, the Cedars, Bernie's Point, the Jetties, under the Cape Pogue cliffs, and down at the Cape Pogue Gut.

In the more accessible places, Wasque, for example, the amateurs mix with the regulars and sometimes it gets to be a circus, with men and women standing shoulder to shoulder in the surf, crossing each other's lines and causing a lot of tackle, tempers, and fish to be lost.

And if it's a nice day, like this one was, the sunbathers and picnickers also pour out onto the weekend beaches. They park their four-by-fours in clusters, break out the grills, chairs, kites, Frisbees, footballs, and umbrellas, and eat and play until late afternoon. I have, on more than one occasion, seen a swimmer or someone on an inner tube come floating through the Wasque fishing lines, carried by the current of the rising or falling tide. Blissfully unaware or ignoring the fact that they are only inches from a hundred fishhooks, they let the tide carry them through the lines until they finally land far down the beach, having paid no attention to the angry cries of the surf casters.

There are sometimes so many four-by-fours on the weekend beaches that it seems like downtown Edgartown. Ah, for the golden days of yesteryear, before everybody and his dog owned a four-by-four.

Because of the cars and the flocks of people, Zee and I usually didn't fish on weekends except very early in the morning when only the regulars are out. Amateur Hour is not our idea of a good time. But this was not a usual weekend, since we had obligations to our guests, so the next morning, after cleaning up last night's dishes, I put two extra rods on the roof rack of the Land Cruiser, an extra tackle box in the back, and ice in the fish box. Then Zee and I made sandwiches for four and stuffed them, with chips, half-sour pickles, beer, wine, iced tea, and cookies, into my big cooler. I added two small floating wire baskets and two quahog rakes to our collection of gear. If we couldn't find a place to get some bluefish, we'd go for some littlenecks or steamers. There is never a time when you can't fish for something or other on Martha's Vineyard.

I got into my dashing spandex bathing suit, and Zee slid into her itsy-bitsy white bikini—larger than three postage stamps, but not by much—and after putting on shorts and shirts over this daring beachwear, we were ready to roll.

"No more all-over tans for a few days," I said. "Too much company."

"Alas," said Zee, sliding her feet into her Tevas. They were good-looking feet. Maybe Pushkin had the right idea. On the other hand, Zee's other body parts were equally stimulating.

Quinn and David Greenstein did not make an appearance until well after nine. Both had abandoned their city clothes for shorts and shirts and both looked city pale. June People not yet exposed to the Vineyard sun. We fed them smoked bluefish, red onion, and cream cheese on bagels, washed down with coffee just touched with cinnamon to smooth it out.

"Okay, you guys," said Zee, when they were done, "we've missed two tides already. Time to hit the beach. You can't catch any fish from this porch."

"Sorry to hold you up." David Greenstein had a white-toothed smile. "I was starved. And that was the best night's sleep I've had in longer than I can remember."

"The Island Sleepies at work," Zee said almost shyly. "I'm just kidding you. You can sleep as late as you want to. It's your vacation."

"I'll be up earlier tomorrow." Again the flash of those white teeth. I wondered if he'd also won the Tchaikovsky international smiling competition. It seemed likely.

Zee's smile was just as bright. "If you plan on swimming, which is a good thing to plan, you'd better put on a bathing suit."

"I've already done that. I was so advised by Mr. Quinn."

"You lay out a winning breakfast," said Quinn, wiping his lips and ogling Zee. "Did I ever tell you that if you just had a lot of money I'd consider using my famous Irish charm to win you away from this guy who claims he's your fiancé? I'm sure he'll never appreciate you as much as I do."

"I did have a lot of money once," said Zee, "but I don't have it anymore. It's too bad you weren't here last weekend, when I was rich. You missed your chance."

"Bad timing has been a Quinn family curse," said Quinn, getting up and starting to clear the table. "Tell me everything."

David Greenstein got up and started helping.

"You don't need to do that," said Zee. "You're guests."

"Yes they do," I said. "If we're going to get down the beach before noon, we've got to get started."

"I used to do this all the time when I was living in Evanston," said David Greenstein. "If I had time to cook these days, I'd still do it." He piled plates on plates, and hooked fingers through the handles of coffee cups, and headed for the kitchen, followed by Quinn.

We were in the Land Cruiser driving south before Quinn got back to the issue of Zee's fleeting riches. While we crawled through the A & P traffic jam, she told him her tale.

"And the bank says it was a computer glitch, eh?"

Zee nodded. "My hundred thou was there for the weekend, but was gone on Monday. That's all I know. Sic transit moolah. I presume that means our relationship is over. Sigh."

"Oh, I don't know," said Quinn. "Maybe we can still work something out."

Going on through Edgartown, Zee played travel guide for David Greenstein. She pointed out Cannonball Park, so called because of its six-inch muzzle-loading cannons and its stacks of twelve-inch cannon balls, and confessed that she hadn't the slightest idea why the cannon balls and cannons weren't the same size.

"Why is that?" she interrupted herself to ask me. Zee sometimes thinks, or pretends to think, that I know more than I do.

"It's like those big vee formations that geese fly in," I said. "One arm of the vee is almost always longer than the other one. You know why?"

"I'm not sure that I want to hear this," said Zee, suddenly suspicious. "Oh, all right. Why?"

"Because the long arm of the vee has more geese in it."

"Haw!" laughed Quinn. When he was really amused, he put two haws in a row.

"That's how it is with these cannons and cannon balls," I explained. "They aren't the same size because the cannon balls are bigger than the cannons."

Zee, who was sitting beside me in the front seat, turned back to David Greenstein. "Now you see what you've gotten yourself into. A week of jokes like that and you'll be begging to get back on the recital circuit."

"I've heard worse," he said. "In fact, I've told worse. Maybe we can have a bad joke contest sometime. Of course Quinn won't be allowed to compete because he tells the worst jokes in the world and would win hands down."

"That's because I'm an ace reporter for the *Boston Globe*," said Quinn. "My whole career is a joke. Compared to me, you guys are just amateur jesters."

We took a right on Pease Point Way, rolled past the cemetery and the fire and police stations, and drove on out toward Katama. The road was full of mopeds whose riders were headed for South Beach, and the bike path was full of bikers going the same direction. It was a beautiful sunny day, so I thought all of the travelers had the right idea.

Zee kept up her travelogue as we drove down past the farm on the great plains, the condos and new houses by the Herring Creek, and, at the end of the pavement, through the crowds of cars, bikes, and people at the beach. I slipped into four-wheel-drive and we headed east over the sand toward Chappy.

We drove along the inside track, following the south shore of Katama Bay. There were clammers and quahoggers in the bay, and a lot of four-by-fours parked or moving along the beach. It was a busy day. To our right, along the ocean shore, the air was full of kites. Still, the beach was uncluttered compared to the places where two-wheel-drive vehicles could go.

There was, as expected, a huge gathering of trucks and Jeeps down by the clam flats near Chappy. The families belonging to them lolled under beach umbrellas or were busy getting sunburned as they heated their grills, flew their kites, and tossed their footballs.

"The movable feast, also known as the portable parking lot," Zee explained to David Greenstein. "One of the ironies of being an islander is that you never have time to enjoy the place the way the tourists do. All week, while the tourists are touristing, the islanders are working. So on weekends they make it up, and come down here to party."

We passed onto the Wasque reservation, going along the narrow road through the dunes, past Swan Lake, where once or twice we've seen otters swimming among the ducks, geese, and swans, and out onto Wasque Point. There, the four-by-fours were parked side by side while beyond them the fishing rods were bending.

"Fish!" cried Zee, pointing. "They're getting fish, Jeff!"

Indeed they were. A lot of people were on, and others were up at the Jeeps, taking fish off their lures.

I swung over and drove along behind the parked trucks. I didn't see many that I recognized. Most of the regulars had moved out. The dozens of fishermen standing shoulder to shoulder, making their casts, were almost all amateurs. Crossed lines seemed to be the order of the day. A lot of fish were being caught, but a lot of gear was being lost, too. I looked at Zee and raised a brow.

She shook her head. "Zoo city. You'd take your life in your hands trying to fish in that crowd. Let's keep going."

Quinn said, "How about trying the yellow shovel?"

"Okay," I said.

"The yellow shovel?" asked David Greenstein.

Zee explained. "The yellow shovel is a spot on the beach. Years ago, we knew a guy named Al Prada who got a kick out of picking up toys he found lying on the beach. I guess he had boxes of the stuff in his garage. Anyway, one day we spotted him fishing just up East Beach a way, in a place we don't normally fish. He had a fish on, so we stopped and got a couple ourselves. It turned out that he'd stopped because he'd spotted a kid's yellow plastic shovel lying on the sand, and while he was there, had decided to make a few casts. Ever since then, that spot's been the yellow shovel."

"Of course, the yellow shovel itself is long gone," I said. "In Al Prada's box of junk, probably."

"But the spot's still there," said Zee, "and we get fish there now and then. We're going to give it another shot now. The chances are there won't be a crowd, and we can introduce you to the joys of surf casting without running the risk of having some greenhorn hook us instead of a fish."

"I'm a greenhorn myself," said David Greenstein.

"No, you're a Greenstein," said Quinn.

"Not down here," said Zee. "Down here he's my cousin Dave from New Bedford. Right, Dave?"

"Sounds good."

"You speak any Portuguese, cousin Dave?"

"Sorry. No Portuguese. Does that mean I can't be your cousin any longer?"

"Not a bit. My own brothers can't speak Portuguese, and I'm getting worse at it every year. No, you'll pass, with or without the language."

"I know French and some German and a little Yiddish. Will that help?"

"A Yiddish-speaking Portagee, eh? Well . . ."

"Okay," said Dave. "No Yiddish."

We arrived at the yellow shovel and got out.

Dave looked around. "How do you know where you are?"

"You just drive along until you're there," I said. "You've read the sign: There ain't no other place that looks like this place, so this must be the place."

"Ah."

"You do this a couple of times, and you'll know," said Quinn.

We got the rods off the roof. My rod and Zee's are eleven-and-a-half-foot graphites with Penn reels. Mine doesn't have a bail. My other rods are fiberglass, also with Penn reels. Zee had and I had Roberts plugs on our lines, and I'd put Spoff's Ballistic Missiles on the lines of the two fiberglass rods. Everybody had a thirty-inch leader.

Dave hefted his rod and raised a brow. "A little bigger than a fly rod," he said.

"I'll teach you everything I know about these things," said Quinn.

"That shouldn't take long," said Zee.

"Women shouldn't be allowed to fish with the men," said Quinn. "Come on, Dave. We'll go down the beach a way so when we screw up our casts, we won't bother J. W. and his lady friend."

They went off to the right.

Zee made her cast and hadn't taken two turns on the reel when a fish hit her plug.

"Wahoo!" she yelled, and set the hook.

Up the beach, David Greenstein turned and looked at her. I couldn't blame him. He may have been around the world a dozen times, but he had never seen another woman like Zee.

He watched her bring the fish in. His eyes were bright. As she carried the fish up to the Land Cruiser, she glanced at him and grinned. He raised a fist into the air and pumped his arm in a victory signal. She raised her rod and shook it in answer. They both looked happy.

I went down to the water's edge and made my first cast. The plug arched far out and hit with a satisfying splash. But no fish hit the plug as I reeled in.

■ 7 ■

Quinn was not only a good fisherman but a good teacher, and David Greenstein, fly fisherman of yore, was a quick study, so it was not long before Dave's casts were beginning to reach out to where the fish were waiting. And it was not much longer before he had his first hit. His rod bent, but as fast as the fish was on, it was off again.

He shook his head and said a few words I had heard fishermen use before when their fish said good-bye.

"You'll get the next one," said Zee, as she hauled in her third or fourth.

And he did. A few casts later another fish hit his plug, and this time Dave set the hook and brought him in. A nice seven-pounder that fought him all the way to the beach.

"I believe 'wahoo' is the right word this time." He grinned at Zee, and dragged the still-fighting fish up to the Land Cruiser.

By that time there were nine other fish lying in the shadow of the truck, and it was high noon.

"What a relief to finally be able to add one to the pile. I was beginning to think I'd never get one." Dave looked at the fish. "What will we do with them all?"

"First we'll put them in the fish box so they'll stay cool," said Quinn. He cocked an eye at me. "What do you think? We want some more, or will this do it?"

48

"It's up to you," I said. "You're the guests. You want to fish some more, get right at it." I turned to Dave. "None of these will go to waste. When we get home, I'll stuff yours and maybe another one, and bake them for supper. Any others that we have, I could give to some people who like fish but can't make it to the beach, or I could sell. But today I'll fillet the ones I don't cook, so I can smoke them later. So catch as many as you want."

Dave was happy. He looked up at the sun. "How about one more before lunch?" He shook his rod. "Wow! I love it!"

I leaned against the Land Cruiser and watched him go down and make his throw. He was beginning to get some reach on his casts. His line arched out and the plug hit the water with a splash. About four turns of the reel in, a blue hit the plug and Dave was on.

"Wahoo!" He turned his head and looked at us, beaming.

We watched him bring the fish in, and all of us were grinning when he came up to the truck. It's hard not to smile when somebody is as happy as Dave was with that second fish.

"Quinn, my boy," he said, laughing, "this is even better than you said it would be! This guy just about wiped me out. What a battle!"

When you first start fishing, you wear yourself out on every fish. Later, you learn to use your energy more efficiently, although a really good fish can still tire you and a run of them can do you in completely.

"Lunchtime," said Zee. "You need to reenergize."

We rinsed the sand from all of the fish and put them in the fish box, then stood the rods in the rod holders on the front bumper and drove to our favorite spot in the lee of the tall reeds by Pocha Pond. By some fluke, no one was there ahead of us, so we had the place to ourselves.

We put down the old bedspread, and got out the cooler, and dug in.

After a bit, Zee looked at Dave and Quinn and said,

"You two guys have been out in this sun about long enough for your first day. Best if we go back home right after lunch, so you can find some shade."

Wise advice.

"You sound very maternal," I said.

"I'm practicing for after we get married."

"How about taking Dave on the rest of the four-wheel-drive tour, first?" suggested Quinn.

For friends and other occasional guests, I offer two tours of the Vineyard: the two-wheel-drive tour around the island's main roads, through its towns, up to Gay Head and back; and the four-wheel-drive tour out to the far reaches of Chappaquiddick via the beaches. Pocha Pond was about a third of the way along the four-wheel-drive tour.

Zee looked at me. "Why not? It's a beautiful day. And if these guys are in the truck, they'll be out of the sun."

"Right you are," said Quinn, his fair Irish skin already dangerously pink.

"You be the tour conductor," I said to Zee. "I'll scale the fish, then I want to get some stuffers to replace the ones we ate last night. By the time you get back, I should have my bucket full."

"I'll stay and give you a hand," said Dave.

"No you won't," said Zee. "You've been out in the sun long enough already. You can go quahogging tomorrow."

I took the fish box out of the truck and my scaler out of my tackle box. Then, with Zee driving and Dave beside her and Quinn in the rear seat, the others set off up toward Dike Bridge, which lay low against the trees up where the water narrowed.

I scaled the bluefish, then waded out and began raking circles for the big quahogs that live in Pocha. While I raked, I thought about David Greenstein. Sometimes you take to someone right away. I felt that way about Dave. It was clear that Quinn, normally as cynical as any other practitioner of his distrustful trade, felt that way, too. And there was no doubt that Zee did. It would have been hard for her to have felt any other way, since he was her favorite musician and was miraculously right here in the flesh instead of out there on the airwaves or embodied only in a tape or disk.

Still, when I thought of Zee's feelings for him, I felt a twinge of jealousy that I didn't like. I made myself remember a sign that hung above one of the doors in my house. There were two words printed on it: NO SNIVELING. I don't like snivelers, and I was not going to be one. Maybe if Emmy Lou Harris suddenly showed up at my house, I would be as happy and starstruck as Zee seemed to be in the presence of David Greenstein. Besides, what was wrong with being as delighted as Zee was being? Was I grumpy just because another man made her happy? What kind of jerk was I becoming?

I had a bucket of nice stuffers and was polishing off a Sam Adams taken from the cooler when the Land Cruiser came swaying back along the sand track leading from the bridge, passed over the beach at the edge of the pond, and came to a stop.

"Terrific," said Dave, stepping down. "I don't know why you ever go home. I can see why those people out on Cape Pogue live there. This place is beautiful."

"Fishermen everywhere," said Quinn. "Fish everywhere. What a day. I see you've been busy while we played tourist."

"Home, home," said Zee. "These guys are getting red, and I forgot the lotions."

Brown Zee and brown me needed no lotions, but our pale guests did indeed need some. We packed the gear, put the rods on the roof rack, and went home via the tiny On Time ferry, which transfers travelers from Chappy to Edgartown. It being Dave's first trip to the Fabled Isle, it seemed appropriate that he make a crossing on the On Time, which is always on time since it has no schedule.

As we waited for the ferry and then crossed with the three other cars that filled its deck, lovely white Edgartown sparkled in the sun. Boats swung at their moorings and anchors in both the inner and the outer harbors, and other boats crossed in front and behind the ferry, passing through the narrows linking the inner harbor to the sound. On the top of the town dock, tourists leaned on the railing and looked at the boats. Fisherfolk sat beneath them between the pilings and trailed their lines in the water.

"Dynamite," said David Greenstein.

Zee gave him a warm smile. She thought it was dynamite too. So did I, for that matter. It's hard to beat Martha's Vineyard on a summer day.

We stopped at the Midway Market for gasoline and a *Globe*. The policemen and golfers who gather at the Midway for early morning coffee and gossip had long since dispersed, but the parking spaces were still jammed with cars. Summer had definitely arrived.

As we drove home, Quinn leafed through the paper until he found what he was looking for. A short note in the Arts and Entertainment section reporting that the eminent pianist David Greenstein had been taken ill and had not appeared at Symphony Hall, as scheduled. His manager assured the public that Mr. Greenstein would soon be back in the public eye, although it was uncertain whether he would perform tonight.

"You see?" said Quinn. "No problem."

"Until tomorrow," said Dave. "Or Monday, or Tuesday."

"Don't worry about it," said Quinn.

"I'm not worried about it," said Dave. "That's why I've got a manager. I pay him a lot to worry for me. I'm not even going to think about music for a while. I feel the way I used to feel when I played hookey from school, and I like it. Guilt mixed with freedom. Heady stuff."

"That's the ticket," said Quinn approvingly.

"That's how I feel about money I owe," I said. "I figure that the guy I owe it to is the one who should worry, since he's the one who doesn't have it. No need for both of us to be in a stew."

"You don't owe anybody any money," said Zee.

"That's what's infuriating about you. You're the only person I know who doesn't owe anybody a cent."

"The secret of my success is not to buy much," I said. "I catch my own fish, I go clamming, I have my own garden, my dad left me my house and land, and this truck is umpteen years old and paid for, like everything else I own. It's not hard to be out of debt if you don't buy anything." I put my hand on Zee's brown thigh. "What's more, I'm about to get hitched to a woman with a steady job, and that means not only no debt, but money in the bank."

"A lot you know about women," said Zee, patting my hand. "I come with built-in costs you can't even guess." She turned to Dave. "Actually this island is an expensive place to live. Everything has to be brought in by boat, and because it's hard and expensive for people to get over to the mainland where they can get bargains, island prices get jacked up to the sky. It takes a good deal of money even to be poor on Martha's Vineyard. We've got one of the highest winter unemployment rates in the state, and the welfare lines are pretty long. Jefferson, here, is the exception to the rule. There aren't many people on this island who don't owe anybody money."

"I make a lot of money," said Dave. "More than I can spend. But I can remember what it was like when I was a kid. We were always sailing pretty close to the wind."

"Don't let the chamber of commerce hear that 'more than I can spend' part," I said. "They'll be glad to show you how to get rid of your dough."

"Heck," said Zee, batting her lashes, "I can show him how to do that all by myself."

"Wait a minute, wait a minute," said Quinn. "This guy is my mark, not yours. I didn't bring him down here so somebody else could rip him off! Get back there, Mrs. Madieras! Back, girl! You've already made your choice of men, however foolish that choice was, considering you could have had me."

"I'm my mommy's boy," said Dave. "She owns my heart and soul. If you don't think so, ask her."

"Your mom's okay," said Quinn. "A little possessive, maybe, but okay. I admit that she thinks I'm a bad influence, but, hey, no hard feelings. She's proud of you, my lad! It's too bad none of her friends know anything about classical music, otherwise they might know what she's talking about when she brags about you."

We drove down my sandy driveway and unloaded in front of the house. I carried the fish box back to the bench behind my shed, where I do my filleting, and got to work.

Dave came out and I showed him how to take the fillets from the bones. He wanted to try it, so I let him. He did all right, considering it was his first time. When all of the fish were filleted, I threw the bones back into the oak brush so the bugs and worms and birds would have something to eat, and took the fillets into the house. In a few days, the fish bones would be bare. Meanwhile, the southwest wind would carry the smells away from the house. The oak brush back there was thick with fish bones.

Zee was already out of the shower, and Quinn was in. Dave was next, and I was last. The outdoor shower is one of man's great inventions. No steamy mirrors, no worry about splashing the walls or dripping on the floor. By the time I got out, the others each had a piece of the *Globe* and were reading and drinking beer. It seemed like a good plan, so I joined them.

Dave was reading the business section. "Hey," he said suddenly, "here's a story about computers and payrolls. Listen to this. 'Money is deposited over telephone lines. The coded messages to withdraw from one account and deposit in another are so brief that they may take less than a second to send. The problem is that if the message is garbled at either end, the wrong amount of money may be sent or the money may end up in the wrong account.' " He looked at Zee. "That sounds like what happened to you last weekend."

"The bank said it was a computer glitch," nodded Zee,

who was brooding over the sports page, wondering once again what was wrong with the Red Sox.

"It's not always a glitch," said Dave. "It says here that it's possible that a clever computer person might, for instance, send a coded message that would indicate that money had been received when in fact it never had been sent. That if all of the messages making up, say, a payroll were diddled with, the thief might be able to funnel a fortune off into some other account and get away with it."

"Sounds too easy," said Zee. "I'll bet they have computer cops to catch those guys. Anyway, you know it wasn't me who funneled that hundred thou into my account, because if it had been me, I'd have taken it out in cash and I'd be spending the money down at the Harborview right now, being waited on hand and foot by devoted servants, instead of here with you characters being entertained with the sports pages of the *Globe*."

"Nonsense," I said. "Here you are surrounded not by paid lackeys, but by ardent admirers ready to heed your slightest whim. Nothing could be better for you. What's more, tonight you get to eat a supper that I'll personally cook. The Harborview has nothing comparable to offer."

"Well, all right," said Zee. "I can be happy here. But only if I get the crossword puzzle. Who's got it?"

"Rats," I said, and handed it over.

But I was thinking about what Dave had said, and later I read the article myself. Interesting, even to a computer illiterate like me.

■ 8 ■

I wondered if being computer illiterate was going to prevent me from becoming a successful twentieth-century criminal. It seemed likely. If not that, some other flaw in character or talent would forbid such ambition. Oh well.

I mixed up some stuffing, put it between bluefish fillets, and put the fillets in the fridge, where they would keep until suppertime. While I was there, I got myself a Sam Adams.

"I thought you stuffed the whole fish," said Dave, who was watching from the kitchen door and drinking a beer of his own.

"That's one way to do it. This way, though, you don't have to mess with the bones."

"Ah."

"Every trade has its tricks. For instance, did you know that you can boil lobster in your microwave, and save all that messing around with a big pot of water on your stove?"

"You don't have a microwave."

"No, but one comes with Zee when we get married. She has a television, too. She comes fully equipped."

"She does indeed. Does she have a camcorder? If she has, you can film your lobster cooking in your microwave, then watch it all on your television set."

"It'll probably be good for me to enter the twentieth century before it ends."

The telephone rang. It was Tony D'Agostine calling from the police station.

"I thought you might be interested to know the results of the autopsy on the Ellis girl," said Tony.

"I am. Something toxic, I presume?"

"Very toxic. It's got a scientific name I can read but not pronounce. I wrote it down." He read a Latin-sounding name that I couldn't understand. "Or something like that. Its English name is water hemlock."

"Like Socrates drank?"

"Nah, I think that's some other kind of hemlock. Don't ask too much from me. Poisons aren't my specialty. Anyway, it seems that this water hemlock grows wild around these parts. In swamps and places like that."

"How'd she get it in her system?"

"She ate it. The medical examiner says there's no doubt about it."

"Suicide?"

"Probably not. Suicides usually don't go out for rides on their mopeds while they're waiting for the poison they took to kick in."

"A point well taken. Murder?"

"Not likely. According to the doc, poison plants aren't too dependable as murder toxins, because it's hard to know how much of the plant it's gonna take to do the job. Big people need more than kids. Healthy people need more than sick ones. That sort of thing. No, this looks like an accident. The girl ate some water hemlock roots and died before anybody could help her. The doc said that people do that sometimes, thinking the roots are eatable. Maybe some kind of carrots or potatoes, I guess, or maybe ginseng, whatever that is. Anyway, he said a lot of people have been poisoned by this stuff. First time I've heard of anybody dying from it here on the island, though."

"How'd she get the roots?"

"We're going to try to find out. We'll talk to her room-

mates and her friends, and see if we can track down the
source. We don't want to lose anybody else."

"No."

I hung up, and remembered the girl wobbling along
on her moped with a frowning face that I'd believed then
was caused by angry thoughts that kept her from being
really pretty, but which I knew now was from the sick-
ness unto death. I thought that she had probably gotten
so sick that she knew she needed help and, seeing my
driveway, had turned in, trying to get to the house she
knew must be there. But sandy roads and dying moped
drivers do not mix well, and she had fallen. She had
willed herself to her feet and staggered on, sicker by the
second, until, finally, her last strength took her off the
driveway, where she fell and died.

Had she cried out? Some last cry that no one heard?
Had she known she was dying? Feared it? Welcomed it
at last as an escape from overwhelming pain?

I felt a touch on my arm and looked down into Zee's
great dark eyes.

"Are you okay?"

I looked around. Dave and Quinn were looking back
at me.

"I asked you what the call was about," said Zee, a
note of worry in her voice. "Are you all right? Was it
bad news?"

"I'm fine. No, it wasn't really bad news. Just strange."
I told them what Tony D'Agostine had told me, and
about seeing the girl on the highway just before she died.

"Water hemlock." I could see that Zee was running
her poison knowledge through her mind. As a nurse, she
knew a lot more about such things than I did. Finally,
she shook her head. Water hemlock was apparently not
included in her mental files.

I looked at my watch. Plenty of time.

"I'm going down to the library," I said. "I'll be back
in time to cook supper. You're all welcome to come
along."

"Not I," said Quinn. "I've had a busy day. It's nap

time for Mrs. Quinn's little boy." He yawned to prove it.

"And I'm going to pick some peas to go with the bluefish," said Zee. "Then I'm going to do some weeding in the flower beds."

"I'll come with you, J. W.," said Dave. "I like libraries."

I, too, like libraries. They're full of books and other interesting sources of information and entertainment, and they're run by people who actually like their work and want to help you, which is to say that they're exactly the opposite of the people who work for the Registry of Motor Vehicles.

Dave and I finally got through the horrendous mid-afternoon coming-home-from-the-beach traffic jam in front of the A & P, and made it downtown. At the four corners, I hung a left on North Water Street, Edgartown's most prestigious avenue, avoided hitting a number of pedestrians who seemed oblivious to the fact that they were walking on a street where real live cars were driven, and actually found a parking place only a block beyond the library.

On ahead of us, the great captains' houses marched toward Starbuck Neck. I pointed out to Dave that the fronts of all of the houses were just slightly out of line with the street, being tilted, as it were, a bit more toward the sea.

"Why were they built that way?" asked Dave.

A good question, but one I could not answer. Another Vineyard mystery yet to be solved.

In the library, Dave wandered and I went to the card catalog and looked up poisons. There weren't a lot of entries, but there were enough. I found the books and an empty chair and began to read.

Water Hemlock. Scientific name: *Cicuta maculata*. No wonder Tony couldn't pronounce it. Also known as beaver poison, cowbane, and locoweed, and by other names as well. Found growing wild in eastern North America and other places. Different species found throughout the United States and Canada, mostly in wet or marshy ground. Grows up to seven or eight feet tall. Jointed stems, purple spots, and small white flowers.

I tried to remember if I'd ever seen a seven-foot-high plant with jointed stems, purple spots, and small white flowers. I didn't think I had. I thought that if I had, I would have remembered it. Purple spots?

Because toxicity decreases as the plant gets older, most poisonings occur in the spring when the plant is young. The whole plant is poisonous, but the roots contain the greatest concentrations. These are sometimes mistaken for parsnips, Jerusalem artichokes, or other edible roots. The poison is soluble in alcohol and chloroform, among other things. Cows have been poisoned by water contaminated with the juice of the plant, and children have been poisoned by making pea shooters and whistles from its hollow stems.

Water hemlock is the most violent plant poison in the United States. A piece of *Cicuta maculata* one centimeter in diameter can cause a fatal poisoning. Death is by respiratory failure or cardiac arrest, and comes between twenty minutes and ninety minutes after ingestion of the poison. It is preceded by stomach pain, nausea, vomiting, diarrhea, labored breathing, weak pulse, and convulsions.

I thought again of the last minutes of Kathy Ellis's life. Gone was any hope I might have had that she had died without pain. Kathy had died in terrible agony, all alone. Beside *my* driveway.

After a while I read some more.

Treatment consists of removing the poison by gastric lavage or emesis with activated charcoal, and by artificial respiration with oxygen to prevent respiratory failure. Treatment of cardiac arrest is also employed, and injections of morphine or barbiturates are used to control convulsions. With early and adequate therapy, the death rate should be less than 10 percent.

Less than 10 percent. But there had been no early therapy for Kathy Ellis.

I leafed through the book and was astonished to discover that I had a lot of poisonous plants right in my yard: rhododendrons, mountain laurel, azaleas, and rhubarb, to name a few. Shocking. When Zee and I began to produce small Jacksons, we would have to be very careful about what they ate along with their allotted square yard of dirt.

I looked at my watch ($6.99, from Trader Fred's. A medium-priced timepiece by my standards. I never go above $9.99). It was time to get home and cook supper. I pushed back my chair and went to find Dave. He was dozing in the magazine reading room, having been overtaken once again by the Vineyard Sleepies. On his lap was an opened copy of a magazine with a computer on the cover. I touched his shoulder and he was immediately awake.

"Time to go home. The call of the evening martini can be heard."

He put his magazine back and we walked out.

"I didn't know you were a computer person," I said.

"I'm a key banger by profession," he replied. "I have a little laptop that I can carry around the world in my travels. It's got a software program that lets me compose on it. Very neat for a guy in my business. I can work on a plane or in my room or wherever I am."

"So you compose, too."

He shrugged. "I'm a performer more than a composer, but, yeah, I do some writing, too. Everybody wants to write something."

"I didn't notice a computer when you brought in your gear."

"Ah, that's because I didn't bring it with me. Mr. Quinn's advice. He said to bring nothing that would let me work. Concentrate on being lazy for a few days." He flashed his grin. "Good advice. But he didn't say I couldn't read. Things in the computer world change so fast that you're always behind the times."

"They say that as soon as you buy one, it's already out of date."

"That's about right." He gestured at the street. "That's what's so good about being down here. Here, nothing much changes. Your place doesn't look like it's any different than it was fifty years ago. The things you do—fishing and clamming—don't change. The tides and the weather are eternal. Your whole life is outside of time, sort of. It's a good kind of life for me, right now. I need some of this before I have to go back to the clock ticking and the schedules and all."

We drove up North Water Street and slowed in front of the refurbished Harborview Hotel to look at the Edgartown lighthouse and the boats in the outer harbor. I pointed out the distant needle that was Cape Pogue Light, which he had visited earlier in the day, then hooked through Starbuck Neck and caught Fuller Street back down to where I could cut right to Pease Point Way and drive onto Main Street and out of town.

When we got home, Quinn and Zee were already on the balcony with hors d'oeuvres and a bucket holding ice and a bottle of Stoli. We joined them, and looked out over the garden and pond to the sound, where sailboats were leaning in toward port as the sun got low.

"Not too bad a view," said Quinn.

True.

"You're in a mood," Zee said to me.

I had been trying to get Kathy Ellis out of my mind. I almost but not quite wished that I hadn't learned how hard she'd died. Now I willed her away and put a smile on my face.

"I'm okay," I said. "Did you know that your cousin here plays with computers as well as pianos?"

"No, I didn't." She smiled at him. "It's good to have a backup trade in case the bottom falls out of the music biz."

"You will be interested to learn," said Quinn, "that even I now write on a word processor. Still with two fingers, admittedly, but no longer on the old standard

Royal. The end of an era. I sometimes wonder what will happen to the fourth estate if the electricity goes off."

"Back to hand-set print," said Dave. "Just like the good old days. Broadsides and pamphlets. No more of these big gray newspapers that nobody reads anyway. We'd all be better off."

"Just because you don't play an electric piano doesn't mean that the rest of us don't need the old kite and key power," said Quinn. He lifted his glass. "On the other hand, none of us need it for this kind of work." He took a drink and sighed with satisfaction.

"I've been thinking about that error in Zee's account," said Dave, sipping his Stoli. "If we get bored this week, we might nose around a little bit and try to find out how that happened."

"How can you do that?" asked Zee, immediately interested. "The bank said it was just a glitch."

"Glitches usually happen for a reason. Most of the time they're human error, like airplane crashes. Maybe we can find the human."

"Do you think so?"

He shrugged. "Probably not. But maybe."

"Anyway, it all got cleared up before anybody got hurt, so what difference does it make?"

"Don't you want to know?"

"Well . . ."

I left the balcony then and went downstairs to do some cooking. Supper was stuffed bluefish, fresh peas, and boiled potatoes topped with breton butter. The wine was cold Chablis. Delish! We ate at the table out on the lawn while we watched the sky darken and the first stars come out.

Another beautiful night on the beautiful island of Martha's Vineyard.

Later, my arm around sleeping Zee, I found myself again thinking of Katherine Ellis. It was the wrong time for such thoughts, and I was awake for longer than I wanted to be.

■ 9 ■

At five o'clock the next morning, we were at Wasque Point nailing the blues as the sky was brightening over Nantucket. The fish were only three quarters of a cast out, and were hitting about every other throw. They seemed to prefer poppers, so that's what we were giving them. There were three other trucks between Wasque and Leland's, and everybody was doing well. By the time the sun climbed up out of the water, we had a lot of fish under the truck. I was taking a coffee break and listening to the classical station over on the Cape when Dave came up from the surf with another nice nine-pounder. I watched as he unhooked the fish and tossed it under the truck with the others.

He clenched and unclenched his fingers and rubbed his arm. "Man, this is great, but it can wear you out."

"It's always a problem. Should you hang in there and kill yourself to get your limit while the fish are still hitting, or take a break and hope they'll still be there after you rest up?"

There was a narrow band of clouds just above the horizon, and the sun was rising behind them. The clouds were shot with fire. I pointed out the tiny irregularity on the horizon that was Muskeget, the little island off the western tip of Nantucket.

"Ah," he said. "Nantucket. Whales, Captain Ahab, and like that. A nice island, but a lot different than this one. Not so many trees, for one thing. Low and gray, but beautiful. I was out there a couple of years ago. Just for part of a day. Flew in, took a bus tour, walked around town, and flew back to Boston."

That was more than I could say. My father had first pointed out Muskeget to me when I was five years old, but I had never made it to Nantucket. Hawaii, Japan, and Vietnam, yes; Nantucket, no. Next month, though, I'd make a visit. With Zee, aboard the *Shirley J.*, on our honeymoon. That was a nice thought, so I held it while I finished my coffee.

By that time, the weekend four-by-fours were streaming in from the west, and Wasque was getting crowded. I went down and got another fish, then came back and started loading blues into the fish boxes. All told, we had almost thirty fish, mostly eight- to ten-pounders. A very nice haul. I put my rod on the roof rack and poured another coffee. On the radio, they were playing something baroque. Not Bach, but somebody else. Who? Telemann? Vivaldi? Somebody in a cheerful mood, at any rate.

Zee saw my rod go on the rack and made one more cast. About halfway in, a fish started following her lure, swirling and snapping at it, but missing again and again. I could see her laughing as she slowed her reel, then speeded it, then slowed it again so that the fish could have a lot of chances. After you've gotten enough fish, it's more fun, sometimes, to have one chase you and miss than to catch him. This one tried once too often, and hit the lure just outside of the breakers. An easy victim. Zee only had to haul him in about thirty feet to land him.

When she got up to the truck, she was happy.

"What could be better? A beautiful morning, and lots of fish!"

"Get some more, if you want."

She looked at the trucks gathering along the beach and at the others still coming.

"No. Zoo time is about to start. We have plenty of

fish. Let's head for home. You have a market for these?"

"I'll give a few away, and sell the rest. I'll take you all home first."

"I love you," she said, standing on her toes and giving me a kiss.

"I love you, too," I said, and kissed her back.

Quinn and Dave came up from the surf. "Shameless, both of you," said Quinn.

"Time to go," said Zee. "It'll be wall-to-wall fishermen here in a little while."

Once we cleared Chappy, we drove west along the outside of the dunes, throwing our shortening shadow in front of us. It was early, and the beach was empty of people. Twenty miles ahead of us, we could see the distant bend of land that marked Gay Head, the far end of the island. The sky was still without much color, and the ocean stretched away to the horizon on our left. It was a lonely and lovely place to be.

Just before reaching the paved road, I cut over to the Herring Creek, and scaled and gutted the half dozen fish I planned to give away.

In town, I stopped at the Midway Market for a Sunday *Globe*, then went on. At home, I unloaded everyone else, then drove back downtown and sold all of my fish except the ones I'd cleaned. The price wasn't too good, because there were a lot of blues around, but I didn't care, since that was what I had expected. I delivered the cleaned fish to four widows and two old couples who liked bluefish but couldn't catch their own anymore, and headed home.

It was turning into a beautiful day, and I felt lazy and good, the way you do after a successful early morning fishing trip. I had made some money and hadn't had to fillet a single fish. I was in high cotton, as they say down South. Happy as a clam at high tide, as they say up North.

When I got to the house, I found Dave sleeping in a lounge chair in the yard, under my big umbrella, and Quinn nodding off on the couch on the screened porch.

Quinn got one eye open long enough to register my arrival and to grunt, then floated back to oblivion.

Zee looked up from the crossword puzzle and put a finger to her lips. "It's good for them," she whispered. "They can both use as much rest as they can get."

Some people on vacation feel guilty about going to sleep because they're afraid they're wasting their money or their time. I prefer the wisdom of some sage I once read about who was quoted as saying that the only difference between a Zen master and anybody else was that the Zen master ate when he was hungry and slept when he was tired. A wise bit of advice, and one that a lot of nonhuman animals seem to take to heart. They don't wait until a certain time of day to eat or a certain time of night to sleep. Instead, they follow the path of the Zen master. Babies are the same way, but adults are not. Down we forget as up we grow, as the poet observed.

So I approved of my guests snoozing, and took advantage of it to read the Sunday paper.

You can probably skip a couple years' worth of Sunday papers and not miss a whole lot, since the news is mostly the same. The Red Sox, weak down the middle as usual, and with a shaky pitching staff as usual, were still in the thick of things, as usual. Baseball is a wonderful game because over the years the very best teams just barely win more than they lose, and the very worst teams barely lose more than they win. Thus, your team always has a real chance. Unless your team is the Cubs, of course.

The Arts and Entertainment pages do change as new shows come into town and old ones leave, but since I rarely go to shows, that news is usually of no great interest to me. Today, the item noting that pianist David Greenstein was still incommunicado did catch my eye, in part because its writer raised the questions of just where Greenstein might be and why was he there instead of performing, as he was supposed to be doing. Reporters are a suspicious lot, and this one, while not really saying that anything was out of whack, was suggesting that maybe it was. I thought that Dave might have a lot of explaining to do when he got back to civilization.

On the other hand, looking at him sleeping in the morning sun, totally unwound, one arm hanging down so that his fingers touched the lawn, I thought that this escape of his was probably exactly what he needed, whether or not he would eventually have to face a hostile press or public. There was something childlike about him as he slept, something innocent and pure. I had seen that same look on Zee's face as she slept, but I had not noted it on a man's face since those faraway and long ago days when young comrades in Vietnam had managed to nap between the cries of havoc and the howling of the dogs of war.

Zee put down her puzzle and came to me.

"Let's go for a walk," she whispered.

I got our crooked walking sticks. Mine was cut long ago when my father and I had a who-can-cut-the-crookedest-walking-stick contest, which I had won by dint of a wonderfully serpentine oak branch that I shaped into a perfectly bent and twisted cane. After that day, I did not take walks without my crooked stick, and I had lately shaped another one for Zee, which was crooked indeed, and crooked enough, though not so crooked as my own.

Crooked sticks in hand, we left our sleeping guests and started through the oak brush toward the Felix Neck Wildlife Sanctuary. An old deer trail led northwest through the trees behind my house. After winding over my land and other people's land, it finally hooked up with the road leading into Felix Neck. It was a good trail for single-file walking, and allowed us to avoid most of the poison ivy and thorns that grow in those woods.

When we got to the Felix Neck road, we could walk side by side at last, and talk as we walked. We headed down toward the barn, then walked back out to the highway and down the bicycle path toward my driveway.

"You know," said Zee, "next weekend is the last weekend I'll get to spend with you until after we get married."

"Because of Mom?"

"Yes, because of Mom. She'll be coming down a few days early to help me with everything, and she'll be staying with me, so I have to live at home."

"And Dad and your brothers?"

"Yes, they'll be coming down, and my sisters-in-law, too. But only a day or so before the wedding, because they all have to get back to work."

"The whole family. All of the Muletos of Fall River. I'll finally meet the gang."

"I probably should have taken you home and introduced you. But they'll like you, I know."

"Naturally. Everybody likes me. I'm a likable guy." But I wasn't a doctor, like Zee's first husband, with whom, Zee had once told me, her mother, unlike Zee, still got along very well.

"And I hope you'll like them," said Zee.

"I hope so, too. But I'm marrying you, not your family."

"Maybe so, but take a good look at my mother before the big day, because they say that the woman you marry will end up looking like her mother."

"Your mother must be a great beauty, then."

She hooked my arm with hers and pulled us together. "What a silver tongue. I'm sure Mom will be as charmed as I am."

"Did I ever tell you that before I changed the names out of sheer modesty, J. W. stood for Just Wonderful."

She let go of my arm, and whacked at my stick with hers. "Thank goodness I still have time to change my mind about this wedding!"

"I still plan to show up." We strolled on. "What'll we do if it rains?"

"If it rains, we'll just move inside John's house. It's big enough for everybody. There aren't going to be that many people."

I thought about John and Mattie Skye's big old farmhouse. We could probably get everybody in the library. Then I started counting heads: Zee and six other Muletos, me, my sister from Santa Fe and her husband; that was ten; the minister, John and Mattie and the twins; that made fifteen. Hmmmm. Then there was Aunt Amelia Muleto, and there were Manny and Helen Fonseca, the chief and his wife, Tony D'Agostine and his wife, George and Margo Martin, and Hazel Fine and Mary Coffin and the other musicians. Good grief. Our little wedding was getting huge.

I glanced at Zee. "Do you know how many people are coming?"

"Probably no more than fifty, all told."

"I didn't know I knew fifty people. Am I supposed to be doing much to get things ready? If I am, I haven't heard about it."

"You just get the *Shirley J.* ready to sail, and make sure you have your getting married clothes rented, and have the ring, and have your best man . . ."

"John is going to be my best man."

"I know. And Mattie is my matron of honor, so it'll all be in their family."

"I think we'd better burn incense or something to persuade the rain gods to go somewhere else for the day."

"I thought you were supposed to sacrifice a virgin."

"Did you ever try to find a virgin on Martha's Vineyard in the summertime?"

"Don't worry," said Zee. "It's going to be a perfect day for a perfect wedding."

"For perfect us."

"That's perfectly right!"

"And you can get everything ready in just three weeks?"

"There'll be Mom and me and Mattie Skye and probably some other people working at it. We'll get it done."

"Zeolinda Jackson," I said. "It has a nice ring to it."

She grabbed my arm again. "Yes, it does!"

We walked along the bike path and turned down my

driveway. I showed Zee the place where Katherine Ellis's moped had fallen. Although a lot of feet had walked
over the sand since that day, some of Kathy's staggering
footprints could still be seen. When we got to the spot
where she had died, we paused.

I wondered if I'd have had the character to make it so
far before I died.

"Look," said Zee, pointing.

I could see a bit of paper beneath a blueberry bush. I
walked over and saw that it was the corner of an envelope mostly covered by leaves. I picked it up and
looked at it. It was a Vineyard Haven National Bank
envelope, and it had been slit open. Inside I found Kathy
Ellis's bank statement and her returned checks.

She had a balance of $750.34. Pretty good for a Vine-
yard summer worker in June. Most college kids working
on the island were lucky to break even by the time they
had to go back to school.

What was really interesting was that during the past
month Kathy had made out eleven checks to cash for
nine thousand dollars each, and another for one thousand dollars even. That added up to a nice round one
hundred thousand dollars, which was *really* good for a
Vineyard summer worker in June.

■ 10 ■

I handed the envelope and its contents to Zee. She looked at them.

"What do you think?" I asked.

"I think that one hundred thousand dollars is a popular number lately. Where does a college student get a hundred thousand dollars?"

"Maybe she was faster on the uptake than you were, and when the computer glitched and put a hundred thou in *her* account, she took it out before the glitch could be corrected."

"Maybe she was rich." She put the checks and the statement back in the envelope.

"Nah. Rich girls have straight blond hair that comes to their shoulders, and they walk like they're carrying hockey sticks."

"Good grief. Here." She handed me the envelope.

"The way I see it, Cash ended up being the rich person. Good old Cash. Let's see if he got it all or if several people got nine thou apiece."

I took out the checks and looked at the endorsements. They had all been deposited in the Zimmerman National Bank in Hyannis by a Cecil Jones for the New Bedford, Woods Hole and Nantucket Salvage Company. Cecil Jones was Cecil Cash, apparently. Or maybe it was really the New Bedford, Woods Hole, Nantucket and Cash Salvage Company. I suggested this possibility to Zee as we walked down to the house.

"I don't think she got her hundred thou because of a glitch, like I did," said Zee.

"Why not?"

"Because she wrote those checks out a few days apart, over a period of a couple of weeks. I think they would have corrected their glitch before then."

"I know everybody thinks that I'm only marrying you for your bod, but it's your brain that won my heart."

"She must have been a rich girl," said Zee. "There are a lot of them down here in the summer, and not all of them have straight blond hair that comes to their shoulders. I'm sure that some of them are very good workers and save their money."

"And make hundred-thousand-dollar payments to salvage companies?"

"Maybe she was buying stock or something. What do you know about money?"

She had me there.

When we got home, Dave and Quinn were awake, so we had lunch out on the lawn table.

"The perfect place for sloppy eaters," I said. "It doesn't make any difference if you get crumbs on the floor." Then I told them about the checks and the bank statement. "What do you think?" I asked.

"I don't think when I'm on vacation," said Quinn. "I only think when I get paid to do it, so call me next week when I'm back in Boston." He leered at Zee. "On the other hand, I'll be glad to think about you for nothing."

"Now calm down," said Zee, patting his hand. "I don't want you to hurt yourself."

"I think it sounds like money laundering," said Dave. "Isn't there some law that says a bank has to report transactions of more than ten thousand dollars to some agency or other? The IRS, maybe, or some banking commission? So that drug barons and people like that can't just deposit hundreds of thousands without anybody knowing about it?"

Zee nodded. "Thus, eleven under-ten-thousand-dollar checks that add up to one hundred thousand dollars, instead of one hundred-thousand-dollar check that the Zimmerman National Bank would have to report. Makes sense to me."

"What do you think?" I asked Quinn.

"Like I told you," said Quinn, "I don't think about things like that while I'm on vacation. It's a beautiful day, and I believe that Dave should have the two-wheel-drive tour while the visibility is good enough for him to see Noman's Land and Cuttyhunk from Gay Head. I'll take him in my car so he won't get any more bruises banging around in that old Toyota of yours. Why don't you get a new truck, for God's sake? That thing must be twenty years old."

I sneered. "How much do you still owe on that chunk of Detroit iron? And how far down the beach can you get with it? You just lay off my trusty Land Cruiser."

Dave and Quinn drove off, and Zee and I stripped to our skins and went out into the yard to perfect our tans, finish the paper, and listen to the Red Sox win a close one at home. By the time Quinn's shiny new car pulled back into the yard, the game was over, we were clothed, and I was listening to my tape of the three tenors. As is not unusual when I hear such singing, my eyes were blurry and my nose was running. I think that if I could just once be Pavarotti singing "Nessun Dorma," I could die happy, knowing that my life had been fulfilled.

Quinn and Zee had observed my sentimental responses to singers before, and were kind enough to refrain from comment, but Dave had not. He sat silently in a lawn chair and listened until the tape ended. I blew my nose. "Absolute dynamite," I said, wiping my eyes. "Imagine three guys like that all in the same place at the same time." My voice felt watery.

"I was there, you know," said Dave. I looked at him, and he nodded. "Yeah. I was playing in Rome, and a fan got some of us tickets. It was July 7. We all went out to the baths of Caracalla. A really beautiful, starry night, with a good moon. Six or seven thousand people. We had good seats down in front. And there they were: Carreras, Domingo, and Pavarotti. And Mehta conducting that big orchestra. Unbelievable. I'll never forget it."

I wondered if he could see me turning green. "If I sell my soul, do you think the devil could arrange a rerun and let me attend?"

"No. God was in charge of that one. Old Nick wasn't anywhere around. You've got a tape of it, and that's your blessing. People talk about the good old days, but in the good old days, you wouldn't have that tape."

"You can have the good old days."

"No thanks." He grinned. "Well, maybe I'd like to go back and listen and talk to Mozart and Ludwig Von and some of the others but I wouldn't want to stay there. No, sir."

Quinn came out with glasses and the Stoli bottle in the ice bucket. Zee followed with crackers, cheese, and bluefish pâté. They climbed up to the balcony. I looked at my watch. It was indeed martini time. Dave and I climbed up to join them.

In the morning Zee was gone before my guests were even awake. Back to work at the hospital, then home to stay with Mom while they and Zee's women friends put together our wedding.

After she was gone I washed up our breakfast dishes, waited until eight-thirty, still heard snores coming from the guest room, wrote a note and leaned it against the coffeepot, and drove to Vineyard Haven.

Hazel Fine was in her office. Her thick, curly, dark hair was nicely coiffed, and she was wearing a summer banker's suit and low heels. She smelled good. When I tapped on her office door frame, she looked up and smiled. "Come in, J. W. How are the wedding plans coming along?"

"You know as much about it as I do. All I know is that it's happening at John Skye's place and that you and your group are going to be playing the music. My job is to show up, and I plan to do that."

"I'm sure you'll perform splendidly. We're all looking forward to having a fine time. John Skye's farm is very pretty."

"You've been out there?"

"Oh yes. Mattie Skye invited us out to show us the place. A very nice woman."

Indeed she is. The apple of John Skye's eye, and a good friend of Zee.

"I need a favor," I said. "Maybe an illegal one."

She cocked her head to one side. "Name it."

"Can I see a list of all the transactions of a hundred thousand dollars or more that your bank has handled during, say, the last month?"

Her gray eyes narrowed. "A curious request."

"That's why I'm talking to you instead of somebody else. I'm trying to exploit our friendship."

"Does this have anything to do with that odd experience Zeolinda had at the ATM a week ago? The hundred-thousand-dollar glitch?"

"Maybe. Maybe more than that. I'm not sure."

"Can you tell me any more?"

I couldn't think of why I shouldn't, so I told her about Kathy Ellis's bank statement and checks.

She tapped her desk with a pen. "And you're wondering how a college girl came up with all that money."

I nodded. "First a hundred thou goes in and out of Zee's account, then another hundred thou goes out of Kathy Ellis's. It's none of my business, but it's made me curious."

She thought awhile. "We can look at the information here in my office. Will that be okay?"

"Are you going to get in trouble over this?"

She gave me a wry smile. "What people don't know won't hurt them. Besides, it's a lot easier to apologize later than to get permission first." She touched a button on her desk and leaned toward a speaker. "Eddie, can you come in here a minute?"

Eddie came in, and Hazel introduced us. "Eddie's our programmer," she said.

Eddie was about twenty-five. He had a pleasant, intelligent face and slightly buck teeth. Hazel told him what she wanted.

"For the past month?" he asked.

"Yes. Can you do that?"

"No problem. Take me about fifteen minutes."

He went out the door.

He was back in eleven, printed papers in hand. He smiled at Helen, proud of his magic machine. "Is that all?"

She smiled back. "For now. Thanks, Eddie."

"Piece of cake." He left, and Hazel gestured to me to close the office door. I did that, and she spread the papers across her desk.

Numbers are not my specialty, but with Hazel's help I began to see what was there. There were two lists. The first was a listing of transactions of one hundred thousand dollars or more, and I was surprised to discover that there had been as many as there were, since the Vineyard Haven National was not a large bank. Apparently they were fairly commonplace rather than rare, as I had imagined. No wonder banks paid little more than routine attention to them. I was also surprised by the size of some of the transactions. The largest was for a bit over nine hundred and fifty thousand dollars, and there were several for a hundred thousand or more.

The second list consisted of the names and addresses of the holders of the accounts involved. The nine-hundred-and-fifty-thousand-dollar transaction turned out to be a real estate deal, and island businesses accounted for the others. Except for one.

There was no record of how Katherine Ellis had gotten one hundred thousand dollars in her account.

On the other hand, there was the one nonbusiness-related transaction. On the Thursday after Zee's hundred thousand dollars disappeared from her account, and the day after Kathy Ellis died, a one-hundred-thousand-dollar check had been written on the account of another woman. A Ms. Denise Vale. I memorized her address and phone number, and pointed to the transaction.

"Can I look at this check?"

"Yes, that might be interesting. I'll be right back." Helen went out of the office. When she came back, she was frowning thoughtfully. "Take a look."

She gave me the check. It was made out to cash and had been deposited by Cecil Jones in the account of the New Bedford, Woods Hole and Nantucket Salvage Company in the Zimmerman National Bank in Hyannis.

I pointed this out to Helen. "What do you think?"

"Bankers are supposed to be a careful lot," she said. "We don't like to jump to conclusions. So far, there's nothing here that doesn't look perfectly legal."

"But?"

"But it's interesting that both Kathy Ellis and Denise Vale each had checks amounting to a hundred thousand dollars made out to cash, and that those checks ended up in the same account over at the Zimmerman National. Excuse me again." She left and came back with a file card. "Guess what?"

"What."

"Denise Vale is twenty-three years old. Another college girl, according to one of our male tellers who has an eye for young women and says he's chatted with her. She still has about a thousand dollars left in her account, by the way."

Like Kathy Ellis, Denise Vale was apparently good at saving money. Maybe she got a lot of tips. A whole lot. "How do you know how old she is?"

"When you open an account, we need a photo ID and your Social Security number. Usually we get a driver's license. We keep the information on file, so we know who we're dealing with, and we check the Social Security number with a central bureau so we'll know it's real. If we didn't do that, people could open up accounts under as many names as they wanted, and could stash away money—stolen money, for example—that no one could ever find. You could rob a bank, stash the money somewhere under an assumed name, and keep it even if you got caught. The authorities could never trace it."

"So now we have two college girls with big bank accounts."

She nodded. "And that *is* unusual enough to make me curious."

"There's no record of large deposits being made in Denise Vale's account," I said. "Only this one withdrawal."

"I'll have to look at the records for smaller transactions. I'll check the transactions in Kathy Ellis's account, too. We know that she was careful to make withdrawals in amounts less than ten thousand dollars, so probably her deposits were in smaller amounts, too. It'll take some time."

"I wonder if Denise Vale knew Kathy Ellis."

"I wonder. They both seemed to know Cecil Jones, whoever he is."

I stood up. "Maybe I'll ask her."

"Let me know what you learn."

"I will." As I went out, I wondered if Denise Vale lived in a swamp. It seemed unlikely.

▪ 11 ▪

I walked out and along the street until I could look
down into Vineyard Haven harbor. There, swinging
at their moorings inside the breakwater, were some of
the loveliest boats on the island, including the large con-
tingent of schooners that always caught my eye. The
Shenandoah was headed out to sea, the square rig on her
forward mast set broad to the following southwest wind,
her decks filled with passengers bound for Nantucket
Sound. The breeze that rippled the waters and filled the
Shenandoah's sails touched my cheek with a gentle
breath. It was a lovely day, but out of my memory came
long-forgotten lines that were in sharp contrast to the
beauty before me:

> *On the trees no leaf is seen*
> *Nor are meadows growing green,*
> *Birds build no nests, no song is sung . . .*
> *. . . For Jesus Christ does punish well*
> *The land wherein the wicked dwell.*

Where had that sad song come from? I dug back in
my mind, but found no answer. I walked on to the Land
Cruiser.

Denise Vale lived in Oak Bluffs. Or at least she had a
post office box there. Her home address was Swan Lake,
New York, but here she had only the P.O. box. I could

80

hang around the P.O. until she showed up to get her mail, or I could do something else. I went to the post office first and found her box, just in case she was standing there or if I ever needed to know where it was. She was not standing there, so I tried the something else: I found a phone and asked for her number. I could not imagine a college girl without a telephone. Sure enough, she had one, and when I told the operator I was with the police, she told me where the phone had been installed. I told her we appreciated her cooperation, turned and said, "Okay, McGillicuddy, let's go," and hung up.

I had never actually known anybody named McGillicuddy, but I imagined there must be one somewhere, so why shouldn't he (or she) be on the same police force I was pretending to be on? I had once been a member of a real police department, the Boston P.D., but if there had been any McGillicuddys on that force, I had not met them.

Denise Vale did not live in a swamp. She lived in a middle-sized house on one of the unfinished dirt streets leading off Barnes Road, not far from the sailing camp. There was a car with Pennsylvania plates parked in the front yard, and some clutter in the yard that seemed to be the remains of a party, or maybe several parties. Empty beer cans, an upset lawn chair, and an overflowing rubbish barrel were the main clues. Evidence of co-ed inhabitants hung on a line behind the house, in the form of various items of male and female clothing. Like me, Denise and her friends apparently preferred the solar dryer over the mechanical variety.

I parked and went up onto the porch. There were pizza containers, plates of half-eaten food, and more beer cans on the floor. I wondered when the cleanup crew was supposed to arrive. September, likely, in the form of the landlord, after the summer inhabitants of the house were back in school. Teenagers and college types are not noted for their neatness, and this household was apparently no exception.

I knocked on the door.

After a while I heard unsteady footsteps coming, and the door opened to reveal a young man wearing wrinkled shorts and a badly hungover face. He stared vacantly at me and mumbled something.

I asked if Denise Vale was in. His red eyes registered a vague understanding of the question. He shook his head and made a noise which seemed to be a negative.

"She does live here, doesn't she?"

"Uhn." The heavy head nodded slowly.

"But she's not here now?"

"Uhn." The head shook.

"Is she working? Where does she work?"

The young man pawed at his face, as if to wipe away the cobwebs. He smelled greatly of stale beer.

"Not here," he said with surprising clarity.

"Is she at work?"

He thought about that, husbanded his strength, and said, "Don't know."

"Where does she work?"

This was a puzzler. He frowned and bit his lip, then raised a feeble finger and pointed in several directions. "Town. Fireside."

"The Fireside, in Oak Bluffs?"

"Uhn." He seemed perilously close to falling over. Then he recovered and looked intently at me. "Missed the party," he said.

Yes, I had. "Thanks," I said. "Get some rest."

"Uhn."

He lurched out of sight. I pulled the door shut and drove back to downtown Oak Bluffs.

Oak Bluffs' main street is Circuit Avenue, which is lined with shops catering to the day trippers who come over on the boats from the Cape. These visitors catch buses at the dock and take tours of the Vineyard. When they get back to Oak Bluffs, they grab some fast food, buy made-in-the-Orient souvenirs with the words "Martha's Vineyard" written on them, and go back to America having "seen" the island. Thousands come and go every summer.

The citizens of Oak Bluffs, knowing which side their bread is buttered on, make no bones about catering to this thrifty day trade, and the little shops and fast-food joints that line Circuit Avenue give the town a honkytonk quality that differentiates it from the island's other major towns: Edgartown, whose captain's houses are huge and white and whose shops are the expensive kind, and Vineyard Haven, which is a normal New England town that just happens to be set on Martha's Vineyard.

Oak Bluffs is not only a street of souvenir shops, of course. It has its share of fine homes, and is famous for the Victorian gingerbread houses that surround its Tabernacle. As a major East Coast black summer resort, it is also the most racially integrated town on the island, and has been for decades. Its black merchants, lawyers, professors, butchers, bakers, and candlestick makers are at least as aristocratic as their white equivalents in Edgartown and elsewhere, and many of their families have been coming to the island just as long.

Oak Bluffs is also home to the Fireside Bar, one of the principal watering holes for the year-round working stiffs and the summer college crowd. The Fireside is where the island's fights usually used to start, and occasionally still do. It is a bar where the smell of grass is mixed with that of beer and various glandular emissions, and a place where an efficient waitress who doesn't mind roving hands and unimaginative proposals can earn a good dollar in tips. It's also where my sweet, half-witted friend Bonzo earns his daily pittance with a broom and a bar rag.

Bonzo was once a promising lad, I'm told, but long before I met him he reputedly got into some bad acid that did a number on his brain. Since then, he has been rowing with one oar. He lives with his widowed schoolteacher mother, loves birds and collects their songs on his recording equipment, and is a childish but dedicated fisherman whenever he can get someone to take him to sea or to the beach. I am occasionally that someone.

I parked up toward the market and walked back down

to the Fireside. The street was crowded, and I wondered once again why these people were here instead of at the beach. Come to think of it, why was I here instead of at the beach?

The Fireside was dark and not too crowded. It served pub food as well as drinks, and the noon crowd was just beginning to wander in. I went to the bar and ordered a Molson. The bartender served me, then went down the bar and began setting out pickles, boiled eggs, pickled sausages, pretzels, and peanuts. I watched the room in the mirror and saw Bonzo cleaning tables in the back. He hadn't seen me yet. An aging waitress began to take orders at the tables.

The beer was good, but then there is no bad beer. Well, actually, there is some bad beer, but Molson doesn't make any of it. When the bartender seemed satisfied with his work down the bar, I waved at him and he came back. I ordered another Molson. When he brought it, I asked him if Denise Vale was around.

He rubbed the bar with a clean rag, and decided that he would tell me. "No," he said. "She's not around."

"I thought she was working today."

"She don't work here anymore, buddy."

"I just went by her place. A guy there said she was here."

"Well, she's not. Dammed college kids. Can't trust a one of them. Don't know what it means to have to work, you know what I mean?" He looked angry.

"Maybe I do," I said.

"You a friend of hers?" His voice was hard.

"No, but I want to talk to her."

"Well, she's not here." He leaned on the bar and looked at me. "Damned kid hasn't showed up for three days. She was supposed to work all weekend and never fucking showed up at all. No telephone call, no explanation, no nothing. Left me shorthanded on the busiest nights of the week. You see her, you tell her she's fired! Had to get my wife in here to fill in. She's still here, for Christ sake. Pisses me off, you know what I mean? Kids

nowadays, you try to give them a break, a job where
they can make a couple of bucks, and what do they do?
They just take off. You know what it is, don't you?"

I could guess what he thought it was. "Spoiled rotten?
No respect for money? Rich daddies? Don't have to
work like ordinary people?"

"That's it, buddy. You got it." He shook his head.
"Seemed like a nice kid, too. Worked real good right up
to now. Then this. Jesus, it's hard to stay in business with
the kind of help you get these days."

"She's a good worker, then?"

"Yeah. Till now, that is."

"Never did anything like this before?"

"No, but once is enough. I got to have dependable
help. I got to be able to rely on my people."

"Like Bonzo."

He glanced at Bonzo, then back at me. "Yeah, like
Bonzo. You know Bonzo? I guess everybody comes in
here knows Bonzo. Yeah, like Bonzo. Bonzo ain't got
much going for him, but what he's got he brings to
work. Every day. He can work here as long as he wants
to. I'll always have a place for him."

"What kind of a girl is Denise Vale?"

"Well, I thought she was okay, till now. You know.
Worked hard, never got too mad, took all that crap the
guys give a girl and never took it personal. I thought I
had a winner. Now this. Now I got to get another girl,
and who knows what she'll be like? I tell you . . ."

"Maybe she's sick," I said. "Maybe she's in the hospital." I thought of Kathy Ellis. "Maybe she fell off a
moped or something."

"You think so?" He was willing to consider it. I got
the notion that if Denise Vale was sick, she could get her
job back.

"I don't know," I said.

The waitress, who apparently was also his wife, came
up with drink orders from the tables, and the bartender
got busy filling them while she took the food orders back
to the kitchen. I looked into the mirror and saw Bonzo

coming toward me. He was wearing his amiable smile. I turned on the stool, and he shook my hand.

"Thought I saw you, J. W. I was busy back there, but I like to keep my eyes open, and I saw you sitting here. How you doing?"

"I'm good, Bonzo. You want a beer?"

His face got serious. "Oh no, J. W. I'm on duty. I never drink any beer when I'm on duty. I got a lot of work to do here. I got to be on my toes."

"Say, Bonzo, do you know a girl named Denise Vale? She was working here last week."

His dim eyes brightened a bit, and he nodded his head slowly. "Oh yeah, J. W., I know Denise. She works here. She gives me some of her tips when I clean up her tables for her. I guess Denise is okay."

"She was supposed to work here over the weekend. Do you know why she didn't?"

Bonzo rolled his eyes toward the bartender and lowered his voice conspiratorially. "Bob's pretty mad about that. About Denise not being here. You know, he had to get Jackie to come in here and work, and they were both pretty mad. And I didn't get any of Jackie's tips, either. Not one. But you know what?"

"What?"

He winked. "I don't think that Jackie gets many tips. Not like Denise does." His voice came back to its normal level. "Denise gets a lot of tips." Then he leaned toward me. "Why you want to know about Denise, J. W.? You a friend of hers?"

"I just want to talk to her. Does she have any special friends here? Somebody who might know how I can get in touch with her?"

He thought carefully. "You mean like somebody who comes in here to have a beer?"

"Yeah, someone like that. Anybody who might be able to tell me where I can find her."

"You mean, like somebody who comes in here to eat, and they and Denise got to be friends?"

"Yeah, Bonzo, somebody like that."

He leaned upon his broom and gave the matter great consideration. Finally he looked at me and shook his head. "I don't know of nobody like that. I guess I'm as good a friend as she's got. She always gives me some of her tips, you know."

"Does she have a boyfriend, Bonzo?"

That was a poser, and Bonzo gave it his best thought. Finally he nodded. "You know, J. W., I think she does have one. She said once to me, she said, I'm going to meet my boyfriend after work and we're gonna go to Falmouth to the movies. Yeah, that's what she said, and that means she's got a boyfriend." He looked at me with his innocent, empty eyes and nodded again. "Yeah, I guess that Denise has got a boyfriend all right."

"You really like the young girls, don't you, you son of a bitch?" said a furious voice beside my right ear. I turned my head to see who was talking and a mule kicked me in the jaw. The world turned odd colors and shapes, and I went off my barstool, over or through Bonzo, and down onto the floor. There was a roaring in my ears, and things went dark, then lightened again. Bonzo was half under me. I rolled off him and looked up. A rhinoceros was walking toward me.

▪ 12 ▪

I got a hand on a barstool and threw it at the rhino's legs. He kicked it aside and came on, but by then I was on my feet. I felt airy, and knew that I was hurt and needed more time. I backed down the bar, touched something on it, and threw the something at the rhino. He ducked and kept coming on. Things were coming back into focus. The roar in my ears became the sound of alarmed and interested voices, and I saw that the rhino was Miles, the medic who had tended to Kathy Ellis's body. His face was red and angry and the knuckles on his left fist were bloody. I faded away from him and touched my jaw. My hand came away red.

I shook my head and Miles came in a rush. He was a big guy. I grabbed a dish of peanuts off the bar and threw that in Miles's face. Salt in the eyes might help.

He came on and threw that left again. I got away from most of it, but slammed into a table. I felt a sharp pain where I still carried that bullet next to my spine, a souvenir from my Boston P.D. days. Normally I didn't think much about the slug, but now the pain sent a rush of fear through me. The table stopped me long enough for Miles to get close, land a hard right, and keep punching. He was a head hunter, so I ducked and got my arms up enough to take most of the blows on them. Another left got through and popped my ear, and I fell or was pushed over the table. Miles tossed the table aside as I got up again. I was beginning to feel less ethereal and more angry and frightened.

I could hear Bob the bartender yelling "Stop! Stop!" but Miles wasn't stopping. He came on, and hit me again, and suddenly I felt some control snap inside of me. A red veil fell over my eyes, turning the world crimson. I heard an antediluvian noise come out of my throat, and then I was no longer retreating, but going to meet Miles. He swung those big fists, but I brushed them aside as though they were the flapping of moths' wings, and hit him four times, very hard below the heart. If he struck me again, I didn't feel his blows. Everything was happening very fast, but it seemed that I had more time than I needed. I could plan things and then do them. I hit Miles on both sides of the jaw, then under his left ear, then in the throat, and when he raised his hands I hit him again under the heart, then stepped back and kicked him hard in the groin. He tried to double over and fall, but before he could do that, I got a hand on his belt and another on his shirt, swung him off his feet, and drove him headfirst into the front of the bar.

Then he was on his face on the floor, and there was blood in his hair. I had a knee on his spine, that bloody hair in my hand, and I was bending his head back and back, when I became aware of Bonzo's voice saying, "No, no, J. W! No, no, J. W. You'll hurt him bad, J. W.! Please stop, J. W. It's not good to hurt people! No, J. W.! Don't hurt him!"

I saw hands pushing down on the hand that was pulling Miles's head back, and slowly the red veil fell away and the world became normal in color. The sound that had been in my throat faded and I was panting, pulling great breaths of air into my lungs. I saw that Bonzo owned the hands pushing down on my hand, and that he was trying with his small strength to keep me from breaking Miles's neck.

"No, no," he was saying. "Don't hurt him, J. W. It's not nice to hurt people!"

I took my hand away from Miles's hair and his head

thumped facedown onto the floor. I took my knee off his back, and got up. My whole body was shaking. I wondered if my teeth were showing. My fangs.

Bonzo was in front of me, looking up, patting my arms. "Good boy, J. W. Come on, I think you should have a beer. Come on, J. W., have a beer. It'll settle your nerves, you know. Come on."

He led me away as others gathered around Miles. I took a stool at the far end of the bar, and Bonzo ran around behind the bar and got me a Molson. I took a long pull. The bottle rattled against my teeth.

People were looking at me with a kind of horror. I spied myself in the mirror. There was blood on my face where Miles had hit me the first time, and blood on my ear, and I had picked up some other scratches somewhere along the line. Only the pain near my spine hurt, but I thought that several parts of me might be painful later. The left leg of my pants had a tear in it, and my shirt was stained with beer, blood, and dirt. There was sawdust in my hair. I didn't think I looked too bad, but the people in the room apparently saw something that frightened them. In fact, I was more afraid than they were.

That red veil had fallen before, and I had sworn I would never let it happen again, but it had come out of nowhere, and again I might have killed a man had someone innocent not been there to stop me. Not for the first time I wondered what ancient monsters live deep within us, under the civilized skins we show the world. Under the skin I show to the world. I drank the Molson and waited for the cops to come.

None did, so after a while I walked to the men's room, which, at the Fireside, is identified by a stencil of a little boy trying to button up his pants. Fireside wit. Inside, I managed to wash off most of the blood on my head and ear. When I stopped shaking, I came out. The police still hadn't come.

Miles was sagging in a booth, being ministered to by members of the audience. He didn't look good, but he did look as if he'd live to fight another day. Bob the bartender came up to me very carefully.

"Look," he said. "Everything's cool. Why don't you go home? Bonzo tells me you're a good guy, so let's just resolve this without any more problems. Nobody's called the cops. No need for that. We've got everything straightened up, and there hasn't been any real damage. So why don't you just go on, and we'll all just forget about this."

"What set him off?" I asked.

"Hey," said Bob, in one of those voices people use when they don't want to rile the person they're talking to, "Miles has been having some problems. He's a good man, but he's been having some problems. I think maybe he just made a mistake, don't you know? I think maybe something you said just set him off. But he's a good guy and I don't want any more trouble. Look, the noon crowd is coming in, and this is a busy time for us. Why don't you just go home? Tell you what, you come back any time later, and we'll set you up with whatever you want. Food, beer, whatever. You just leave now, and we'll be glad to have you back later. What do you say?"

"I'd like to know why he came on me like that."

"He's been stressed. You know? Look, I don't want to have to call the cops. Bad for business. You understand? But, Jesus, man, I don't want no more trouble here, and Miles, he's not a bad guy. He's just got problems and I'm afraid he took 'em out on you." He paused. "Or tried to." Then, "Bonzo says you're a good guy, too. Why don't you just go on home and let us all get on with our business. Okay?"

I looked at him, and he stepped back. "I don't want any trouble," I said. "But I want to know what set him off. I was minding my own business when he hit me. I want to know why he did that."

Bob flicked his eyes around the barroom. A lot of people were looking at us. "Listen," he said. "That girl you were asking Bonzo about. Denise Vale?"

"Yeah?"

"That's his daughter. You know? She's tangled up with some guy Miles don't take to. You understand?"

If my brain had been a computer, it probably would have started making little clicking noises.

"Keep talking," I said.

Bartenders hear a lot of sad stories. "What do I know?" asked Bob. "Miles and his wife split a couple years back, and the girl went off with Mom. Broke Miles up. And then, the girl comes back this spring and starts hanging around with some guy Miles don't think shit of. You see how it is? Hey, Miles is an okay guy, but I think this whole bit's flipped him, this business with his daughter. Bonzo said you two was talking about her when Miles clubbed you. Jesus, mister, first I thought he was going to kill you, and then I thought you was going to kill him. I tell you, I never saw anything like that for years. Christ almighty. Now, I know how you must feel, but look around this place. Everybody's staring at you wondering what you're gonna do next. I don't want that. I just want to serve some lunch to these people and have them forget about what just happened. Not that they will, mind you, but you'd be doin' me a favor if you'll just go on home and let all of this settle. What do you say?"

I looked across the room at Miles. He looked as bad as I felt.

"Okay," I said. "Is he all right?"

Bob put a friendly smile on his face. "Sure. Sure, everything's cool. Thanks for being a good guy. Sorry this had to happen. You come back, now. Food and drinks on me. Bring a friend."

I headed for the door. People parted in front of me like the Red Sea splitting for Moses.

Outside, the summer air was warm and fresh. I walked up the sidewalk until I got to the Land Cruiser. Like a lot of fishermen, I keep a small first-aid kit in my truck. After all, many a man has been sliced by bluefish teeth or fins, or has managed to hook himself instead of a fish. I found a Band-Aid and, looking in the rearview mirror, stuck it on the split in my skin where Miles had first hit me. I couldn't figure any way to stick another on my cut ear, so I let that go. I took a couple of aspirin while I was at it, in anticipation of future pains. Then I drove back to Denise Vale's house and pounded on the door again.

When the dazed young man appeared, finally got his eyes focused, and recognized me, I asked him when he'd last seen Denise.

He tried to think about the question, but finally had to give up.

"She wasn't here for the party, was she?" I asked.

"She wasn't?" He frowned. "Yeah, I guess that's right. I wonder where she was." He offered a slack-mouthed grin. "Denise likes to party. Party, party." He became somber again. "I think maybe I had too much party."

"I'm J. W. Jackson. Who are you?"

"Me? I'm Roy."

"Denise Vale has a boyfriend, Roy. Maybe she spent the weekend with him."

The idea seemed to impress him. "Hey, maybe she did."

"Do you know his name?"

"Who?"

"The boyfriend."

"What about him?"

"What's his name?"

"Uhn. Let's see." Roy frowned and scratched his belly. "Roy . . . No, that's me. And you're J. W. Let's see . . . George, maybe? No, that's not it. Rick? Richard? Vance? Something like that."

"Does he have a last name?"

"Uhn. Beats me."

"Do you know where he lives?"

Roy had no idea.

"Are you in college, Roy?"

He yawned and his breath was the fire of dragons. "Yeah. Sure. Princeton."

Princeton. "What are you studying?"

He thought about that and figured it out. "Philosophy," he said. "Philosophy and religion. Economics. Stuff like that. I'm pre-law. Say, what time is it, buddy?"

I told him.

"Jesus," he said. "I'm supposed to be at work, I think. I better take a shower."

I didn't want to discourage him from doing that, so I left and drove back home to see how my guests were doing.

They were doing fine. I found a note telling me that Quinn was giving Dave his world-famous guided tour of Edgartown, but that they'd be home in time for an afternoon dip in the briny before the cocktail hour. And were we going fishing again in the morning?

Why not? There weren't very many mornings when I wasn't happy to go fishing.

I took a shower and then made a pita bread sandwich with the remains of last night's baked bluefish, a slice of Swiss, and some horseradish. Then I found a beer in the fridge and had lunch on the balcony. There was a light east wind, and it felt good. The beach road was lined with parked cars, and the water beyond was busy with boats. On this side of the road, novice surf sailors were taking lessons in the flat waters of Sengekontacket Pond. It was an interesting-looking sport, but I preferred sailing the *Shirley J.*, my eighteen-foot catboat.

I thought about the *Shirley J.* In three weeks I'd be sailing in her with Zee on the way to Nantucket. A sailing honeymoon. It played well in my imagination.

When I was through with lunch, I drove into Edgartown to see the chief of police. My back hurt, but I tried to will away the pain and the worry that went with it.

▪ 13 ▪

Edgartown is a small village, but it has the best-equipped police station on the island, and well-trained personnel. It has a couple of detectives, a fingerprint lab, a photo lab, and other modern accoutrements. Except for the chief, who prefers to keep his old familiar .38 special, its officers all pack modern 9mm semiautomatics. When I was a Boston cop, I also carried an old .38, but times change.

I tried the station on Pease Point Way first, but naturally the chief wasn't there. The department may be modern, but its budget isn't big enough to allow its chief to sit around in his office all day. Besides, who'd want to sit in an office on as nice a day as this?

"He's probably down on Main Street somewhere," said Kit Goulart, who was behind the front desk. Kit Goulart and her husband are about the same size as a pair of oxen, and could probably outpull most of the teams at the annual county fair, if they had a mind to. I pretended to ogle the badge on Kit's large bosom, got a laugh in reply, and went into town.

The chief was strolling along the sidewalk on Main, headed down from the courthouse. Naturally there weren't any parking places on Main, so I drove past him to Water Street, hooked a right, then a left, and parked the Land Cruiser on Collins Beach, just beyond the No Parking sign. Fishermen park on Collins Beach all the

time and don't get tickets because Edgartown is a boat-
ing town, and the police prefer to ignore the local trucks
parked on the sand.

I walked back to Main, passing under the giant Pagoda Tree that some sea captain brought to the island in
a flowerpot back in the 1800's, and wondering once
again how many giant Pagoda Trees there were in the
United States. Had there ever been a Johnny Pagoda-
seed, spreading pagoda trees across the frontier for the
use of future generations? If so, my history books had
overlooked him.

Edgartown's streets were full of tourists wearing
shorts and sandals and pastels. It seemed like the middle
of July, but it was only June. More people every year.
Good news for the merchants, no doubt, but a subject of
constant griping among a lot of year-rounders, who
greatly enjoyed talking about the good old days when
there weren't all these cars and their accompanying traffic jams, when there were still parking places, and when
you could walk downtown and know the people you
met.

I caught up with the chief at the parking lot in front
of the yacht club.

"What do you want?" he asked. "You live up there in
the woods and you never come to town in the summertime unless you have to or you want something from
somebody." He looked at my face. Then he took my chin
in his hand and turned my head first one way, then the
other. "And what door did you walk into? A revolving
one, looks like. You okay?"

"I'll live. What do you know about Miles Vale?"

"What about him?"

"First time I ever saw him was when the medics were
working on the Ellis girl up in my driveway. Since he
was with the ambulance, I figure he must live here in
Edgartown. And since you're the chief of Edgartown's
finest and know everybody and everything that happens
in town, I figured you might know something about
Miles Vale."

"Like I said, what about him? Miles do this to you?"

"What kind of a guy is he? I hear his wife left him, and that their daughter went with Mom. Then, I hear, the daughter came back to the island and started hanging around with some guy Miles doesn't like. That's all I know about Miles."

"Miles do that to your face?"

"Why? Does Miles have a reputation for beating people up?"

"Did Miles beat you up?" The chief was suddenly very official.

"I hear people say Miles is a good guy. Fella up in Oak Bluffs told me that. Tony D'Agostine told me that, too. No, Miles didn't beat me up."

The chief thought for a second. "Did Miles try to beat you up?"

"The last time I saw Miles, he was sitting in a booth in a bar, surrounded by well-wishers. Look, all I want to know is what kind of a guy Miles is. If he's a good guy, why did you think he might have tried to beat me up? Does he beat other people up?"

"Just hold on a minute. First, tell me. If Miles didn't beat you up, did you beat up Miles?"

"Miles is fine." I wondered if he really was. I hoped so.

"All right," said the chief. "You don't talk to me, I don't talk to you. Have it your own way."

"About Miles, now . . ."

"Miles who?"

"Miles Vale."

"Never heard of him." The chief dug his pipe out of his pocket, checked to see if there was any tobacco in it, and lit up. Knowing my weakness, he blew a bit of smoke my way.

I don't miss cigarettes anymore, but the smell of a pipe still makes my nose start to work. Every time I get a whiff of pipe smoke, I decide that I'll break out my corncobs and briars again. They were still in their rack at home, although I hadn't used them in years. I inhaled the chief's smoke.

"You're a mean bastard," I said, inhaling again. He blew some more smoke. "I don't have to stand here," I said. "I can just go home." He blew a smoke ring that disintegrated in the southwest wind. "All right," I said. "Miles took a swing at me up in the Fireside."

"Looks like he connected. Tell me about it."

"You know how these barroom battles go. You push each other around until you both get tired. Nothing much comes of it."

"Who pushed last?"

"Let's call it a draw."

"Why did he swing at you?"

"The bartender says it's because he heard me asking Bonzo about his daughter, Denise. I guess that Miles gets testy when guys are interested in his daughter, so he took a poke at me."

"Why were you asking about Denise Vale?"

"I wanted to ask her a couple of questions."

"What about?"

"I wanted to ask her what she thinks the chances are of the Patriots making the Super Bowl. Denise is supposed to have a boyfriend that Miles doesn't like. Do you know who that might be?"

"Is that what you were going to ask her?"

"Yeah. For one thing. Do you know who the boyfriend is?"

The chief tried another smoke ring. No better luck. He looked up Dock Street, then up Main Street. Cops look around a lot. "You want to get his opinion on the Super Bowl, too, I imagine."

"I'd be happy just to know who he is."

"Well, I can't help you. When Janice left Miles, Denise went with her. The two of them went out to live in her old hometown in New York. The girl went with her mother because Miles never liked any of the boys she knew here. None of them was ever good enough for Miles. Probably he's got one of those Freudian complexes they talk about. Not Oedipus, some other one. The one where Dad doesn't want to let go of his little girl. There must be a complex like that. These psychologists have a name for everything there is and some for things that don't exist."

"But the girl came back."

"Yeah. This spring. But she isn't living with Dad. She's someplace else."

"Up in Oak Bluffs, with a bunch of college kids in a sort of communal house. But she's not there right now. Been gone a couple of days. That's why I was at the Fireside. She works there. I thought somebody might know where she is."

"You know more about her than I do, then."

"I figured she might have moved in with her boyfriend."

"If she did, they better not let Miles find out."

"Do you know who the boyfriend is? Is he some island guy she came back to?"

"I don't know who he is. All I know is what I hear from the other medics who work with Miles. I guess Miles thinks it's some off-island guy Denise met in college or somewhere. Whoever it is, Miles doesn't like him any more than he liked any of the other guys who wanted to date Denise."

"Miles sounds like a sick guy. You can't keep your daughter from having boyfriends."

"What do you know? How many daughters do you have?"

A point well taken. But in fact, since I was about to get married, I had actually given the matter some thought. If Zee and I ever had a daughter, how would I feel about the guys who came to her door? I wasn't even married yet, but already I felt protective of my little girl. So how was I going to feel when she was a teenager, old enough to make a lot of her own decisions? Worse, for sure. Who were these acne-faced characters on my doorstep, anyway? Only one thing on their minds, probably. Maybe Miles was right after all.

"Do you know where Miles's wife lives in New York?" I asked.

"As a matter of fact, I do. Pretty name, that's why it stuck with me. Place called Swan Lake. Not too far from NYC. I guess it used to be one of those borscht circuit resorts, where the city people went during the summer. Maybe it still is. Pretty name."

"Well, well," said a voice, "look who's here."

I turned and found Quinn and Dave walking up. They looked quite touristy in their sandals, summer pants, and pastel shirts. Dave, I noticed, had bought himself one that said "Martha's Vineyard" across the front. Just the kind of guy the tee-shirt shops love to see.

"This is Zee's cousin Dave, from New Bedford," I said to the chief. He and Dave shook hands.

"And this is Quinn, down from Boston."

This time the handshake was shorter and more formal.

"I remember you," said the chief. "That story a while back about the drug bust. Sharp island drug guys and the not-so-smart cops who caught the little fish but let the big ones slip away."

Quinn held up both hands. "That was then, Chief. This is now. I'm on vacation. Besides, I don't remember picking on you. I picked on the DEA guys, as I recall."

"Yeah. Well, they all went home afterward, but some of us live here and had to take the barbs from the local wise guys."

"That goes with the job," said the unrepentant Quinn. "The slings and arrows of outrageous fortune, I think they call that stuff. I never knew a cop that didn't need a thick skin sometimes. No different here than anywhere else." Then he suddenly changed his tone. "Look, Chief, someday I may be down here again on some other story. If that ever happens, I'll want you working with me instead of against me. I want friends on police forces, not enemies. A cop who's mad at me is no help to me. So let me buy you a beer when you get off duty, okay?"

"You made the cops look bad," said the chief, who can be just as stubborn as the next guy.

"No," said Quinn. "They ended up looking bad because they blew the bust, not because of anything I wrote. All I did was report the truth."

The chief was not so fond of the DEA that he wanted to defend its members enthusiastically, so he contented himself with a grunt for a reply, and turned to Dave.

"So you're Zee's cousin, eh? Down for the wedding?"

"Oh no," said Dave. "Afraid not. Got to get back to work at the end of the week. First time down here. Beautiful place."

"Yeah," said the chief. "Say, have we met someplace before?"

"I don't think so," said Dave. "You ever been over to New Bedford? I have a frame shop over there."

"Haven't been over there for a long time. And you've never been here?"

"No, but I'll sure try to get back again, now that I know what the place is like."

"You sure look like somebody I've seen," said the chief. He knocked his pipe out against a light pole. "Well, I've got to meander along. Nice to meet you, gentlemen. You'd better go stick your face in a bowl of liniment, J. W."

He went off toward the town dock.

"He's right about that face," said Quinn with interest. "How'd you get that, anyway?"

I gave him the chief's revolving door theory, but I don't think he believed me. Instead, he gestured toward the Navigator Room.

"What you need is a drink," he said. "On me."

"Two golden words I thought I'd never live long enough to hear," I said. "Lead on."

And in we went.

▪ 14 ▪

The Navigator Room offers its customers Edgartown's finest public view of the inner harbor. There are tables both inside and outside, where you can sit and watch the boats at anchor or going by. At the closest dock you can rent a day sailer or an outboard motorboat, should you be so inclined. Once, when I was in high school, I taught sailing there for a summer. Beyond the dock, not too far out, the *Shirley J.* swings on her stake.

We drank our beers while Quinn unfolded his copy of the *Globe* and showed us the latest story about the increasingly mysterious disappearance of David Greenstein. Local hospitals and private clinics had been approached by reporters. The physicians of the stars had been interviewed. Inquiries had been directed at friends, relatives, and professional associates. No one acknowledged knowing anything. Some people were beginning to suspect foul play. Kidnapping, perhaps? But there was no ransom being demanded.

"What do you think of that ransom bit?" Quinn asked me. "How long will it be before the notes and calls start coming in?"

"Not long," I said.

"What do you mean?" asked Dave in surprise. Then he lowered his voice and leaned forward. "I haven't been kidnapped, for God's sake!"

"Yeah," said Quinn. "We know that, but who else

does? Some people are going to try to make some money out of this before it's over."

"Whenever there's a major crime," I said to Dave, "people who didn't have anything to do with it like to get involved. They'll confess to murder, for instance. There are people up in Boston who confess to every murder they hear about. In this case, somebody or some group is going to send a ransom message saying they've got you, but they'll let you go for X amount of money."

"Good lord," said Dave. "That's no good. What if somebody believes them?"

"Exactly," said Quinn. "That's why we'll have to make a couple of phone calls to assure people that you're fine. One to your manager and one to your family ought to do it. What do you think, J. W.?"

"That should do it. You do the talking, Dave, so they'll know it's really you. Just a few words, so the call can't be traced."

"We'll use a public phone, just in case," said Quinn. "And just to make double sure that everybody knows you're okay, you can call the *Globe* and *Herald* music critics and let them spread the news."

Dave drank his beer and licked the foam from his lips. "Exciting times. I'll try to remember all this the next time I play hookey."

"You just make sure that you get on a slower schedule," said Quinn, in a paternal tone. "That way, you won't get worn out and won't have to do this sort of thing again."

"Gosh, you sound just like Uncle Quinn," I said. "Maybe even Father Quinn."

Quinn suggested that I try a difficult physical act.

We finished our beers and went outside, where we found a public phone right on the back of the Junior Yacht Club. It didn't offer much privacy, but we pooled our change and Dave made his four quick calls while Quinn and I got between him and the tourists strolling by, so no one could hear him. When he hung up the phone, Dave seemed satisfied. "I am alive and well and unkidnapped," he said happily.

I wondered how much background noise had gotten through, and whether it made any difference. Probably not, since street sounds are more or less the same wherever you go. Besides, the people Dave had talked to probably weren't listening to background noises anyway.

Of course, if anybody was taping the calls coming in to those phones, the background sounds might become subjects of professional study. Even then, though, I doubted if they'd mean much. Besides, Dave would be back in public before much longer, probably before anybody could make anything of the phone calls. Dave had been quick with his calls, so I was pretty sure none of them had been traced.

I also had some phone calls that I wanted to make, but I would make them from home.

"Nice town," said Dave. "Great flowers in people's yards, terrific boats in the harbor. A beautiful place."

True. At the four corners, Dave and Quinn took a right along North Water Street on their way to their car and I went left on South Water on the way to mine. I drove home and phoned the hospital. Zee was there.

"How are things?" I asked.

"Things are okay."

"I just wanted to tell you that I think this getting married idea sounds better and better. That way I'll get to talk to you in person instead of over the singing wires."

"I agree." There was a slight pause. "Mom's coming on the six o'clock boat."

"Mom. As I understand it, she's the old-fashioned sort who wouldn't cotton to the idea of me spending any more time up there, or you spending it down here at my place."

"You got it, sweetheart. Until they start throwing rice, it's celibacy city for us, I'm afraid."

"You don't suppose I'll actually explode before that, do you?"

"Try not to!"

"I imagine I'm going to meet Mom before too much longer."

"Ah, I'm glad you brought that up. How about tomorrow night? I'm going to give her a day to get herself all together, and then I think you should come up for supper. Give you both a chance to look each other over. Can you do that?"

"As long as I don't have to wear a tie."

"Wear whatever you like. Six o'clock?"

"Six sounds good."

"How are your guests?"

"We're fishing in the morning."

"Rats. You'll be fishing, and I'll be here with my mother."

"That's what you get for being a bride-to-be. We manly men do not vary our routines for a mere impending marriage."

Zee advised me to try the same difficult physical act that Quinn had suggested.

"I'd rather have you do it," I said.

"Not until the rice flies, I'm afraid. Six o'clock, then?"

"Six it is."

I found a Sam Adams in the fridge and thought about things. Then I dialed Ma Bell and got Janice Vale's number in Swan Lake, New York. It was mid-afternoon, and I wasn't sure that anybody would be home, but a woman's voice answered.

"Mrs. Vale?"

"Yes."

"This is J. W. Jackson. I'm calling from Martha's Vineyard. I'm trying to locate a friend of your daughter, and I thought perhaps you can help me."

She hesitated. "What's this all about, Mr. Jackson? Why don't you just ask Denise?"

"I'm having trouble contacting her. Besides, this is a confidential matter, Mrs. Vale. I don't want to frighten anyone unnecessarily."

"I don't keep confidences from my daughter, Mr. Jackson. Perhaps you should know that before you go on. What's this about, anyway? What do you mean you don't want to frighten anyone? Frighten who?"

"If you want to tell your daughter about our conversation, please do so. Let me explain. Your ex-husband attacked me this morning because he thought he heard me mention your daughter's name. He seems insanely jealous of any man who might be close to her."

"Are you close to her, Mr. Jackson?"

"No. I've never even met her. But Miles Vale didn't wait to find that out. He attacked me, and I suspect that he'll do the same to the young man I'm trying to locate. I don't want to frighten your daughter, but I do want to know that young man's name, so that I can warn him about your ex, and he'll be on his guard. Miles Vale is an unbalanced man, I think. Do you know the young man's name?"

"You mean Denise's boyfriend."

"Yes. I'm told she has one, but I don't know who he is or where to contact him. I think he should be warned. Can you help me find him? I don't know if he's here on the island somewhere, or somewhere over on the Cape."

"That Miles! He's always had that wildness in him. I liked it when we were young, but it didn't take long for the shine to wear off. He's a strange man, you know. He can be kind and loving one minute, and cold as ice the next. And he was always jealous of Denise. Always. I think there's a name for his condition. But then again, he's a medic, and a good one. He's saved more than one life by being good at his job. Did he hurt you?"

"I'll be fine, but I'm afraid the boyfriend won't be, if Miles catches up with him. So I want to catch up with him first. Can you help me?"

"Well, I suppose you're talking about Glen Gordon. He and Denise have been close ever since they met doing that play in Denise's freshman year in NYU. He was a senior, but they hit it off really well, and after he graduated and went to work, they still dated, especially after she had that problem in the dorm and got her own place.

"Glen is a very nice, intelligent young man. I believe he's working with a firm over on Cape Cod somewhere. I'm sure that's why Denise went back to the Vineyard for the summer. So she could be with him some of the time, at least."

"Do you know the name of the firm?"

"Let me think. Oh yes. Frazier Information Systems. I remember because my grandmother was a Frazier. No relation to the information people, I'm afraid. I think they're located in Hyannis."

"Do you know what he does there?"

She laughed. "Oh, I'm sure it's something I wouldn't understand if he tried to explain it to me. You know how these young folks are. To them, computers are as common as salt. But to me, they're a huge confusion. No, I'm afraid I can't tell you what Glen does. Something to do with accounting, or banking I think."

Banking. "He's a computer guy, eh?"

"Yes he is. And not one of those egghead types, either. He's smart as the dickens, but he's just as warm and nice as you could want. A real gentleman. The girls love him, and I don't blame them. He's a charmer. Why, if I was thirty years younger . . ." She laughed.

"Do you know his address, by any chance?"

"No I don't. I'll tell you though, Mr. Jackson, I want you to find him and warn him about Miles. Miles must be twice Glen's size. The boy might really get hurt. Maybe you should tell the police. Maybe they can do something."

"Is there anybody else in Denise's life? Any other guy I should get in touch with?"

"Denise has a lot of friends. She's very popular."

I remembered that the teller at the Vineyard Haven National Bank had certainly taken note of her. "Anyone else who might be special? Anyone Miles might think he should be mad at? Does the name Cecil Jones mean anything to you?"

She thought for a moment. "No, I never heard that name. Of course a pretty girl like Denise attracts the boys . . . Well, you know how young folks are these days."

I wasn't sure that the young folks were any different now than they ever had been, but I didn't say that to Janice Vale. Instead, I thanked her, assured her that I would do my best to locate and warn Glen Gordon, and rang off.

Glen Gordon was a tickle in my brain.

Where had I heard of him before?

Had I heard of him before?

Sometimes late at night I get these little flutters in my memory and they drive me crazy. I can't make any sense of them, yet I can't stop thinking about them. I can't go to sleep, and I hate it. It wouldn't be so bad if, at last, I'd remember whatever it is that's bothering me, but sometimes the little itches and flutters end up not referring to anything at all. They're just little glitches that keep me awake for no good reason. Very irksome.

Fortunately, it was still only mid-afternoon, and although I had cooking to do, I was still able to think about Glen Gordon because in the kitchen my hands do all of that work by themselves, so my brain can do other things. Thus, I thought about Glen Gordon as computer whiz and as somebody who did something or other for banks.

Computers and banks. Denise Vale and her hundred-thousand-dollar withdrawal. Zee and her on again—off again hundred thou. Poor Kathy Ellis and *her* hundred thou. Computer glitches.

Being both a computer illiterate and a man with a permanently unbalanced checkbook, I did not seem to have the tools to make much headway in these foggy realms. Before I could get too lost, Quinn's car came down the driveway and he and Dave got out. Dave unloaded a case of beer, some French bread and Brie, and some hard pepperoni.

"Balcony supplies," he said. "I think we should get right up there and devour this stuff before it goes bad."

That seemed like a much better idea than brooding about banking, so we went right up.

▪ 15 ▪

At five-thirty the next morning a school of big blues moved in to Wasque Point and began to hit. There were several trucks on the beach, but plenty of room for everybody. The rods bent and sang and we walked our fish down under the other rods until we could get them. They were running about twelve pounds and were full of fight.

I was feeling the results of yesterday's brawl. My face was puffy, my ear was sore, I was stiff, and my back still hurt where I'd banged into a table. Ever since the doctors had told me that the bullet was still there, I had wondered now and then whether it would someday move and cause me problems. Now, the pain made me fear that the dreaded day had finally come.

I had received other wounds that had laid me up for a while, but I'd never been afraid of their damage the way I was afraid of the bullet. The surgeons had told me that they were sure that the bullet wouldn't ever change position, but now I knew that I had never believed them, really. What's more, they'd never taken into consideration the possibility that I might someday be knocked into a table by an angry medic.

So my back hurt and I was worried even as I joined the others in hauling in the big blues.

Dave and Quinn worked hard, but had to take breaks between fish, since their surf-casting muscles were not in shape. Bruises, sore back, and all, I was able to keep at it, and by the time the sun popped up just north of Nantucket and flooded the sand and sea with that clear, born-again light, we had a good number of fish under the Land Cruiser.

As I brought up my latest blue, the morning air was warming. Dave and Quinn had stripped off their sweatshirts, and gone back after more fish of their own. I caught a glimpse of my face in the rearview mirror and wondered what kind of impression I was going to make on Zee's mother. I also suddenly wondered if this bullet-near-the-spine business might not make marriage to me a less than good option for Zee. If the damned bullet did move, and if it lamed me or did worse, what kind of life would I be offering her?

I didn't like the thought, and wondered if I was just being skittery because I was feeling a little pain. Or maybe more than a little. Had that hurt and the suppressed fear that went with it been the cause of the red veil of primeval rage that had fallen over my eyes in the Fireside? I've long thought that all anger is a manifestation of fear.

Would my fear someday make me angry with Zee? Would I lash out at her whenever my back ached or I felt some pain near my spine? Or was I just feeling sorry for myself? I thought of the sign over the doorway to my kitchen: NO SNIVELING. Good advice. I pushed my worry away from me and went back after more fish.

Both of my fish boxes were full when Quinn and Dave ran out of steam and we called it quits. The sun was clearing the clouds along the horizon, and the air was clear and warm. The wind was still blowing the watermelon scent of bluefish over the water and into our nostrils.

Dave and Quinn poured coffee and leaned against the hood of the Land Cruiser. I found the Rhode Island C and W station on the radio, and we listened to Tanya sing about her problems with her man.

Dave flexed his fingers and shook his hands. They get

stiff when you're hanging on to a rod and fighting good-sized bluefish. Sometimes at the end of a summer I have a hard time getting my fingers to straighten out completely. When I was young and working as a pick and shovel man on road gangs during vacation, my fingers were sometimes hooks by the time I went back to school in the fall. Dave's hands were the tools of his trade, so he needed to be careful about them.

"How many did you get?" I asked him.

He grinned. "A million, if you count the ones I lost. I think I landed eight. What a morning!"

"That's about a hundred pounds of bluefish," I said. "Not bad."

"It'll help pay for the three plugs I lost." He knotted and unknotted his hands. "Man, it's frustrating to lose them right in the surf. You work them all the way in, and then lose them right there. I even lost one after I got him up on the sand. He snapped the line and was back in the water before I could get to him, leader, plug, and all. Whew!"

He laughed.

"They don't count till they're in the box," said Quinn.

"How many did you get?" asked Dave.

"I don't know," said Quinn. "I lost track. Enough."

"How about you, J. W.?"

"I don't know," I lied. I always know. Between us, we had almost four hundred pounds of fish. That would more than pay for lost gear. "I think that's enough exercise for one day," I said. "We'll sell these guys on the way home."

Waylon and Willy and friends of theirs sang to us as we drove into Edgartown, got rid of the fish, and went on home. There, I dangled the Land Cruiser keys in front of Quinn's nose. "I have things to do, places to go, and people to see. I'm a busy, busy man. You, on the other hand, are just another loafing vacationer. I'll trade these keys for yours, so you and Dave can hit the beach and watch the girls, while I toil to make America great."

"I'll give you a hand at the toil," said Dave.

"It's not real toil," I said. "I'm just going to do a little weeding in the garden, then talk to some people."

"J. W. doesn't do real work," explained Quinn. "He's retired, and lives off our taxes. Come on, kid, let's throw together some lunch and hit the beach. We don't want you showing up back in Boston without a tan." He dug out his car keys and handed them to me. "Can I trust you with an American car?"

"Can an American car be trusted?"

"Farther than you," said Quinn. He squinted at me. "You'd better do something about that face, if you want Zee's mother to have a good impression of you."

"I'm not marrying Zee's mother."

"Don't be too sure."

They left, and I went out and weeded the flowers and the gourds I had growing along the fence. I liked gourds because I had fond memories of how they'd looked in my father's garden, when I was a kid. In those days I was reading Tarzan books, and, although I'd never seen a genuine jungle, I thought the tendrils and leaves of the gourd vines looked like miniatures of the real thing. Not too many years later I had seen a real jungle, but I still liked gourd plants, even though the two weren't much alike. So much for realism.

I picked some pea pods from the garden, and took some of last winter's scallops out of the freezer. I had a woked meal in mind for supper, and you can't start a woked meal with better stuff than fresh pea pods and scallops.

I put the pea pods and scallops in the fridge, and broke out a cold Sam Adams, the sun being over the yardarm in Rio by that time. Then I called the police station, looking for Tony D'Agostine. He wasn't there, of course, but I left a message for him to call me. About a half hour later, he did. I asked him how I could get in touch with Kathy Ellis's roommate, Beth Goodwin. He told me where she lived and where she worked, and gave me her home phone number.

"You having any luck tracking down the source of that water hemlock?" I asked.

"Not yet. Seems like the girl, Kathy Ellis, was sort of a health food nut. Ate fiddleheads and like that. Vegetarian. Cooked her own meals so she wouldn't have to eat what the other people in the house ate and they wouldn't have to eat her stuff. That's why nobody else got sick. She was the only one to eat the hemlock."

"And nobody knows where she got it?"

"So they say."

"How many people were in her house?"

"Just three. The two females and a male."

"Peter Dennison?"

"Yeah. How'd you know that?"

I told him about meeting Dennison and Beth Goodwin in my driveway the day after Kathy Ellis's death.

"Do you believe them when they say they don't know anything about the hemlock?" I asked.

"You were a cop," said Tony. "What do you think?"

I thought that Tony was reserving judgment about who was telling the truth. He didn't believe and he didn't not believe.

"What do you want with Beth Goodwin?" asked Tony.

"I want to ask her about Kathy's financial situation."

"What do you mean?"

I told him about finding Kathy Ellis's bank statement, then about Denise Vale's bank account. I could almost see his ears prick up. "First Zee had a hundred thou for a couple of days," I said. "Then there was Kathy's hundred thou, and then there was Denise Vale's hundred thou. That's a lot of hundred thous."

"It sure is," said Tony. "I don't make that much in a week, including overtime. You still have that bank statement, I think you should bring it down to the station. It sounds like maybe it's evidence. I wish I knew what it was evidence for, though."

I told him I'd bring it down, hung up, and dialed the number he'd given me. I didn't expect anybody to answer, since it was a beautiful day and the college kids on the island would probably be on the beach if they weren't working. To my surprise, a female voice said, "Hello?"

I told her who I was and asked to speak with Beth Goodwin.

"This is Beth. I remember you. What can I do for you, Mr. Jackson?"

"I'd like to come by and talk to you. About Kathy Ellis."

After a moment she said, "Sure. Why not?"

I went into town and left the bank statement at the police station, then hooked back up the Vineyard Haven Road till I found the turnoff that led to the house Beth Goodwin and her friends had rented for the summer. It was an old house in the middle of a new development west of the road that had never quite developed as much as its developers had planned. Like a lot of people, they had presumed that the land boom in the early eighties would last forever, and had overextended themselves so that mostly they had nice curvy roads that were lined with empty lots and only a scattering of large, new houses. Beth Goodwin's house had been there long before the paved roads had been punched through. It was an old farmhouse that was not in great shape, but it brought its owners a lot of rental money during the summer.

There were similar failed developments all over the island, sad mementos of greed and shortsightedness. A lot of money had been gambled and lost during the boom period, further evidence that the wheeler-dealer types and the bankers who financed them were probably as dumb about economics as the rest of us. Somehow that notion always heartened me, since it suggested that my own admitted ignorance about money might be shared by the supposed professionals in the field. Why is it that we like to see the pros go down? The banker go bankrupt, the psychologist go dotty, the priest get nailed by the vice squad?

Don't ask me.

I parked the Land Cruiser and walked to the house. Beth Goodwin met me at the door. She was wearing a robe and carrying a portable phone.

"I'm out back, catching some rays. I have to go to work in an hour, so I didn't have time for the beach. Come on through."

We walked through the house and out into the backyard. There was a rusty table there, topped by an umbrella that had seen better days. The table was surrounded by plastic chairs, the kind you can buy in the A & P for about six bucks. There were two aluminum lounge chairs. Beth Goodwin went to the one facing the sun, took dark glasses out of a pocket of the robe, then took off the robe and lay down. She was wearing a one-piece bathing suit slightly larger than a dishcloth, and had a very nice tan. She looked at me.

"You don't mind, do you? I can talk and tan at the same time."

I didn't mind at all. I could talk and stare at the same time.

"I've told the police everything I know," she said. "I don't know what I can tell you that I didn't tell them."

"Officer D'Agostine tells me that you have no idea where Kathy might have gotten the water hemlock."

"That's right. When I think about that, it scares me. If Peter and I were vegetarians, we might be dead, too! Poor Kathy."

"She bought her own food and prepared it for herself. Is that right?"

"Yes. Even in college, she liked to fix her own food. It was hard for her to find the kind of food she liked in the cafeterias, so mostly she preferred to do her own cooking. The thing that just breaks my heart is that she was the healthiest person I know. She was very conscientious about her diet, and about exercising. And then this had to happen. It makes you wonder."

I thought that Beth looked in pretty good shape herself, but didn't say so. "Where did she shop?" I asked.

"In the A & P, and at the health food stores."

"I heard that she liked wild food. Fiddleheads, and that sort of thing."

"Oh yes. She made sassafras tea from the sassafras trees that grow down near Sengekontacket, and she found lamb's-quarter growing in the old garden over there." She pointed, and I saw that there was indeed an old garden behind a badly listing shed. Part of it was still wild, but some of it was newly cultivated. "Peter and Kathy put in that little garden as soon as we got down here in May. They have lettuce and radishes and things like that. Peter likes to garden."

I remembered that she'd said that when she and Peter had come down my driveway.

"Could the water hemlock have been growing back there by the garden, or down where she got the sassafras?"

"I don't know. I think the police and somebody from the Felix Neck Wildlife Sanctuary tried to find out, but I don't know if they found anything."

Then I remembered something else Beth had said, and a little light flickered in the back of my brain.

I leaned forward. "When you were at my house, you wondered what people would say when they heard about Kathy's death."

"It was awful. Peter and I had to tell her friends, and the people where she worked." She sat up and I saw tears beginning to run down her cheeks. She took off her glasses and wiped at her eyes. "It's only been a week. Sometimes it feels like a day, and sometimes it seems like a year. I'm sorry." She began to cry.

I waited and after a while her sobs lessened. She wiped at her face with the robe.

"I've got to get dressed for work," she said.

"What did the people say when you told them?" I asked.

"They were shocked, just like us. Nobody could believe it."

"How did Gordy react?"

"Oh, that was the worst of all. I didn't know how to get in touch with him, but that night he called Kathy and I had to tell him that she was dead. I think he was more devastated than the rest of us. He asked all kinds of questions and then he seemed to just break down. He couldn't talk and had to hang up."

"Gordy was her boyfriend?"

She nodded. "Yes. Ever since she went to college."

"NYU."

"Yes. We all go to school there. That's where they met. She was a freshman and he was a senior, but they hit it off right away."

"Does the name Cecil Jones mean anything to you? Did Kathy ever mention the name?"

She looked at me with her watery eyes. "No. I never heard of him. Who's he?"

"I don't know who he is. Where does Gordy live now? Where was he calling from?"

She got up and put on the robe. "I don't know exactly. He lives over on the Cape someplace. He'd come over to see Kathy here, or sometimes she'd go see him there. He came over the very next day after the accident and tried to help us get through it. I think he was the one who needed the help, if you want to know the truth." She brushed at a strand of hair. "Look, I really have to get ready for work. I'm sorry."

I got up. "You've been very helpful. When will Peter be home? I'd like to talk to him a bit, too."

"He won't be home until late. He's working in a kitchen and he'll be there until the restaurant closes. You can probably call him late tomorrow morning. He gets up just before noon. You just missed him today."

We walked back through the house. At the front door, I asked her one last question: "What's Gordy's real name?"

"Glen," she said. "Glen Gordon. But everybody calls him Gordy."

"A charming guy, eh?"

She nodded. "He really is. You just have to love Gordy. It almost killed him when Kathy died."

Almost, but not quite. I thanked her for her help and drove away.

■ 16 ■

I still had a little time before getting gussied up to meet Zee and her mother, so I went home and looked up Miles Vale's telephone number. Miles lived in the Dark Woods, up behind the new post office. Feeling as achy as I did, I figured he probably felt worse and would either be at home or in the hospital. I dialed his number. Miles answered. I told him who I was. He hung up.

I dialed again and he let the phone ring quite a while before answering it. Again I told him who I was. This time he didn't hang up.

"What do you want?" he asked.

"I want to talk about your daughter's boyfriend."

"What about him?"

"Is his name Glen Gordon?"

"What of it?"

"Do you know where he lives?"

"Over on the Cape someplace."

"Do you know his address?"

"If I knew the son of a bitch's address, I'd go over there and kick his ass."

"Why would you do that?"

"Because he's fucking around with my daughter, and he's a bastard, that's why."

I didn't think it would do much good to point out that his daughter was a grown-up woman who probably didn't need or want Daddy protecting her from men.

"She never said where he lived? What town, maybe?"

"She doesn't talk to me much. Her mother poisoned her mind against me."

Miles was a sad case. There are other people like him, people who see themselves living in an evil, exploitive world. I think it's a kind of projection; they see other people being petty and vindictive the way they themselves are. On the other hand, Miles was a medic, and apparently a good one. People are more complex than we sometimes remember. He was not a happy man, though, and I thought he was not likely ever to be one. I decided the best way to deal with Miles was to appear sympathetic.

"Listen," I said, "I want to find the son of a bitch myself. I know you thought I was just another guy after Denise, but you were wrong. I'm after this Glen Gordon character. You punched a friend, buddy, not an enemy. But let's forget about that. Anything you can tell me about Gordon, anything at all, might help me find him."

Miles thought about that for a while, then he gave a grunting sort of laugh. "You banged me pretty good, pal. You hurting any yourself?"

Miles was apparently the sort who didn't mind hurting if he knew you hurt too.

A little flattery might grease the wheels. "I have some bruises I didn't have before. You pack a pretty good punch."

"Yeah, I was going good for a while. Then I wasn't going so good." I don't think he knew quite how things had turned around.

I gave him an out. "Hell, I have ten years on you. Besides, I think I got lucky. Let's just not do it again, okay? I think once was enough for me."

He grunted some more. "Me too, buddy, me too. Next time we'll have a beer instead, eh?"

We manly men chuckled at each other.

"Say," he said. "Why you after this guy?"

"Your daughter's not the only girl he's involved

with," I said. "I have my reasons. Let's leave it at that. You know what I mean?"

Miles thought he did. "Well, lemme see if I can come up with anything. Like I said, Denise doesn't talk much to me. Seems to me, though, that this Gordon son of a bitch lives over in Hyannis, or maybe Falmouth. She goes over there to meet him, and he comes over here to meet her. That's about all I know."

"Would you know him if you saw him?"

"Never laid eyes on him."

"Did you ever hear of a man named Cecil Jones?"

"That's a limey-sounding name. No. Who is he? Some other bastard who can't keep his pecker in his pants?"

Sweet Miles. "I don't know who he is. The name just came up."

"Well, I never heard of the guy."

"When Denise goes over to the Cape, does she take the ferry, or the *Island Queen*, or the Hy-line boat to Hyannis?"

I could almost hear him snap his fingers. "Say, that's right! She takes the *Queen*! That means the bastard lives in Falmouth."

Maybe. Or maybe Gordon met her there in his car and they drove off to his place in some other town.

"Do you have a picture of your daughter? If you do, I'll take it up to the dock where the *Queen* comes in and see if anybody on the boat can tell me anything about her. Like if somebody met her on the other side."

This notion seemed to please him. "Yeah. She sent me this picture of her in her dorm in college. It's pretty good. You come by, you can take it, long as you don't lose it or anything like that." Miles had gotten very friendly, it seemed. Compensation for having picked a fight with me?

"I'll be right over," I said.

Miles met me at his door. He looked terrible. He was hunched over and moving very slowly, and his face was puffy and many-colored. He looked at me and grimaced. "Yeah, we got to each other, all right. My mistake. I

thought you were just another guy after my little girl."
He put out his hand. "No hard feelings."

We shook hands. "I'm old enough to be her father," I
said. "Besides, I'm getting married in a couple of weeks,
and one woman is all I can handle at a time."

"Well, I wish you luck, buddy. I was married once
and it turned sour. Here."

He gave me a five-by-seven framed picture of a young
woman. She was fresh-faced and smiling. Her hair was
a light brown and curled down to her shoulders. She
was wearing jeans and a sweatshirt emblazoned with the
initials NYU, and was sitting at a desk. There were post-
ers on the wall behind her, and a pile of books and papers on the desk.

"Don't you lose that," said Miles. "I want it back."

I assured him that I wouldn't, and drove to Oak Bluffs.
I felt sorry for Miles, but I didn't think I'd ever warm to
him.

The boats from Hyannis and Falmouth come into the
Oak Bluffs harbor and load and unload at the dock by
the parking lot, not far from a heavy concentration of
moped dealers that a lot of islanders would like to see
take their business to some other island. It was a nice
day, and I was quite prepared to laze away some time
in the sun, looking at the boats in the little harbor, but
as luck would have it the *Island Queen* was just coming
in through the channel between the stone jetties. The
Queen ferries day trippers between the Vineyard and Falmouth, and makes several passages a day. It provides
fast, comfortable service to a lot of people, but I had
hope that some of the crew would remember a pretty
girl like Denise Vale, who took the boat fairly often.

And such, indeed, proved to be the case. The second
crewman I showed the picture to even remembered her
name.

"Denise. Sure. A dish. We talked. Saw her just last
week, in fact."

"Going to the Cape or coming back?"

He shook his head. "I don't remember. Usually she

went over one day and came back the next. I think she had some guy over there. Lucky him."

"She ever mention his name?"

"If she did, I don't remember what it was."

"Was it Glen Gordon? Or maybe Gordy?"

"Sorry, pal."

"Did she travel alone or with somebody?"

"Alone. I don't think I ever saw her with anybody."

"Did she meet anybody when she got to Falmouth? Was anybody waiting for her?"

He grinned. "I wondered who a girl like that was meeting, so I watched her a few times. She never met anybody. She just walked up the street alone."

"And nobody brought her to the boat when she came back?"

"Nobody I ever saw. Say, what's this all about?"

It was nice to have an honest answer available. "Her dad's worried about her. He's laid up for a while, so I'm doing some legwork to try to track her down. I thought maybe she was with her boyfriend."

"Well, I don't know if I helped you any."

I wrote my name and number on a piece of paper and gave it to him. "If you see her, tell her I'd like to talk to her. If she doesn't want to do that, give me a call. There'll be a couple of bucks in it for you. Her dad's pretty anxious about her."

"You a private eye or something?"

"I have a badge, but this isn't anything official."

That was true. I still had my old Boston P.D. badge, and I was anything but official in my snooping.

"Well, okay. If I see her, I'll have her call you or do it myself."

The last of the Cape-bound passengers were aboard. The gangplanks were pulled, the whistle blew, and the *Queen* pulled away and headed out across the sound to America.

It was a bit past noon when I got to Denise Vale's house. I wondered how Roy from Princeton was doing. Better,

I hoped. Two college-age girls wearing beach robes were getting into a rather spiffy-looking convertible. My friend John Skye, who, between Vineyard summers, teaches things medieval at Weststock College, says that one way you can tell the difference between students and teachers is that students always have newer and more expensive cars. I got out of the Land Cruiser and walked over.

The women eyed me without enthusiasm. It was clear that they were headed for the beach and didn't want to delay their departure.

I put on my best smile. "I'm looking for Denise Vale. Is she here?"

They exchanged looks. Then the nearer one spoke.

"Who are you?"

"J. W. Jackson. Is Denise here?"

A slight pause. "No, she isn't."

"I talked with Roy yesterday. He said she hasn't been here since before the weekend. Do you know where she is? Her father's worried about her."

That seemed to loosen them up a little. "We're worried, too," said the girl. "It's not like her to do something like this."

"We're starting to think of going to the police," said the other girl.

"That might not be a bad idea," I said. "Have you tried to find her? Have you called her mother? Her boyfriend? People she might be visiting? The hospital?"

"The hospital? No, we haven't . . . That is, we did call Glen, but he said he hasn't seen her. He said he'd call if she showed up. Maybe we should call her mom . . ."

"Glen Gordon? Her boyfriend?"

"Yes."

"Can you give me his number? I'd like to talk with him."

They exchanged looks, then the nearer girl got out of the car. "I'll get it for you. He lives over on the Cape."

She went into the house.

"I hear that Glen Gordon attended NYU?" I said.

The girl in the car nodded. "That's where Denise met him. There are a lot of NYU kids down here for the summer."

"I hear that Denise is twenty-three."

The girl was too young to be worrying about her age or anyone else's. When is it that women start lying about how old they are?

"That's right," she said. "She's going to have a birthday next month."

"How old is Glen?"

She thought about that. "I guess he must be a little older. I think she said she met him in school when she was a freshman. He's got one of those faces that look about twenty. You know what I mean. Sort of a baby face." She suddenly grinned. "He's really cute, actually. We kid Denise about him, and tell her that if she ever gets tired of him, to let us know and we'll be glad to take over. She doesn't think it's as funny as we do."

"That kind of guy, eh?"

She made a little waving gesture with her hand and kept her grin. "Well, you know. . . ."

The other girl came out of the house with a piece of paper in her hand. She gave it to me.

"I don't think Denise is with him," she said. "I think that Glen would have had her call, if she was." She put her lower lip between her teeth. "Do you really think we should call the hospital, and the police?"

"It won't hurt," I said, thinking that I should call the hospital myself. "But unless they actually know something about her, the police will tell you that most missing persons are missing because they want to be, or because it just never occurred to them that other people might even think of them as missing." I glanced at the sun. "If you two plan on catching some rays, you'd better get going."

Actually, I was the one who needed to get going, so I thanked them and left.

First I went to the hospital. There was no Denise Vale there. There was no Zee, either. She was home with

Mom, presumably getting squared away for the big wedding. I wasn't sure why it took so much effort to get married, but apparently it did.

I was hungry, but I thought I knew where I could get some lunch and some information at the same time, so I headed for Vineyard Haven.

▪ 17 ▪

Hazel Fine generally went home for lunch. Lunch was always very good, so I didn't mind dropping in just as it was being served. Mary and Hazel, being the nice kind of people they were, could hardly just sit there and eat while I just watched, so they would come up with some food for me, too. It was an old bachelor ploy that everybody knew about, but it still worked as well as ever, so I never hesitated to put it into effect. The fact that in a couple of weeks I wouldn't be a bachelor anymore was not disturbing, since it had been my observation that married men whose wives were away could use the same trick to get free meals from women who felt sorry for them. I suspected that it might be possible for an enterprising man to live a long and good life and never have to buy or prepare his own food.

"Well, well," said Mary, answering the door. "Look who's here. It's the bridegroom."

"Is Hazel here?"

"You know very well she's here. Come on into the kitchen."

I followed her and discovered Hazel attending to a bowl of cold broccoli soup and thin chicken and cucumber sandwiches.

She smiled at me. "J. W. How nice. Have you eaten? No? Well, sit down and join us. There's plenty for all.

Mary, I think we have a bottle of white wine in the fridge. I'm sure J. W. would like some."

"I'm sure he would," said Mary. "Perfect timing, J. W."

"Thank you. Would you believe me if I told you that I really didn't mean to drop in just in time for lunch?"

"No."

"Well, okay, I'll fess up. But that's not the only reason."

She poured me a glass of Chablis and set a bowl of soup in front of me. I tried it. Delish! I love cold veggie soups.

"Is the other reason a wedding issue?" asked Mary.

"Nope. A banking issue." I looked at Hazel. "I've asked everybody I know who knew Kathy Ellis or Denise Vale whether they ever heard of Cecil Jones. None of them know the name."

"Maybe neither girl knew him."

"He's the guy who signed the back of their checks. Two hundred thousand worth that we know of. If they didn't give the checks to Cecil, who did?"

Hazel nibbled on a sandwich. "I don't know. That's one of the things about checks made out to cash. Anyone can cash them. But just because Cecil Jones cashed them doesn't mean that the girls gave them to him or even knew who he was. It's quite possible that they gave them to someone else who passed them on to Cecil Jones." She pointed her finger at me. "That blank expression on your face suggests that you're thinking of something, J. W. What is it?"

I told her about Glen Gordon's link to Kathy Ellis and Denise Vale.

She took another sandwich and nibbled some more. I had one too, and ate it in two bites. "Well, well," said Hazel. "One boyfriend, two girls. Interesting."

"A not unfamiliar tale," observed Mary.

"He met them both while they were at NYU," I said. "Both girls were freshmen when he met them, and he was a senior. The interesting thing is that Denise Vale is three years older than Kathy Ellis."

"Ah," said Mary. "I see. So Glen Gordon was a senior when Denise Vale was a freshman and was still a senior three years later when Kathy Ellis was a freshman. He had a long senior year."

I nodded between spoons of soup and bites of sandwich. "But supposedly he's a very sharp guy, not the kind to need three senior years in order to graduate."

Hazel wiped her lips. "And you say he's an accountant?"

"Denise Vale's mother said that. She really didn't know too much. He works with computers, but that's about all she could say. All of us computer illiterates are pretty fuzzy about what people actually do with those things."

"J. W.," said Mary, "the twentieth century is almost over. I think you should try to at least enter it before it's gone."

"This from a woman who plays eighteenth-century musical instruments," I said.

Hazel sang and Mary played recorders and other out-of-date instruments in an island ensemble specializing in early and baroque music.

"I know some people over at the Zimmerman National Bank," said Hazel. "Perhaps I'll take a little time this afternoon and make some inquiries about Cecil Jones and the New Bedford, Woods Hole and Nantucket Salvage Company."

I emptied my wineglass. "Good. Can you check out Glen Gordon too? I'd be interested if there's a tie-in between him and the salvage company. And while you're at it, you might find out something about Frazier Information Systems. I'd like to know what they do."

Hazel stared at me. "Frazier Information Systems?"

"Yeah. That's where Glen Gordon works, according to Denise Vale's mom. Why the wide eyes?"

The wide eyes narrowed. "Because Frazier Information Systems is the company that's been handling our accounts and is transferring them to our new computer system."

I felt a little tingle inside. "Then maybe you already know everything you need to know about them," I said, not believing it.

She shook her head. "No. This bank was doing business with them when I came to work here. Since I've been here, FIS has always done good work for us, but I really don't know much about them."

We looked at each other. "Then I guess you'll check them and Glen Gordon out," I said.

"I guess I will," she said.

Mary surveyed the empty dishes on the table. "Well, J. W., at least we don't have to worry about what to do with the leftovers. There aren't any leftovers. You're better than a vacuum cleaner."

Because of Vineyard Haven's system of one-way streets, it was faster for Hazel to walk back to work than for me to give her a ride. Instead, I drove home and got things ready so Quinn and Dave could fix themselves some supper. I put out the wok and the cooking oil and the rice, chopped some veggies to go with the scallops and pea pods, and put the soy sauce and Mongolian fire oil on the table. Preparations for a feast fit for a king. It was almost foolproof, too; all they had to do was not overcook things.

While I worked, I ran things through my brain, then stored them away. It was getting crowded up there.

I took an outdoor shower, brushed my teeth and shaved, wondering once again whether I should grow some hair on my face. A handlebar moustache, maybe, or maybe one of those skinny moustaches and little pointed beards that you see in drawings of old-time Mississippi gamblers and such. The bruises on my face and my fat red ear could use a little cover-up, but I would just have to live with them.

Clean and shining, although black and blue as well, I put on my Vineyard red slacks and a shirt with a little animal over the pocket. I wore my blue belt with the whales on it, and my deck shoes without any socks. A pale blue summer jacket topped everything off. Vineyard chic. If it wasn't for the way my face looked, I could probably get into the yacht club wearing this stuff. And all but the shoes were from the thrift shop, too. Not bad. I wondered if Mom Muleto would be as impressed as she should be.

To fortify myself, I had a Sam Adams, America's finest bottled beer.

By the time Quinn and Dave got home from the beach and had showered and changed, I was on my third beer. I showed them the cooking stuff.

"You're on your own tonight, guys."

"No problem," said Dave. "We've never starved yet."

Quinn put a hand on each of my shoulders and then stood back. "A thing of beauty is a joy forever," he said, admiringly, looking at my clothes. "Except for the face, of course."

At five-thirty, I brushed my teeth for the third time that day, and headed for West Tisbury.

I took a right on the Vineyard Haven Road, a left on Barnes Road, and another right on the West Tisbury Road, and headed up-island. I lived down-island, along with the other citizens of the Vineyard's three largest villages. Up-island is so called because the prevailing winds oblige sailboats to tack if they want to fetch the towns at the west end of the island. Since Zee's house was quite a way from the nearest water, you really couldn't sail there, but she was up-island anyway.

As had been Captain Joshua Slocum, the world's first single-handed circumnavigator, who, long ago, had owned a place not too far from Zee's house.

I went through the center of West Tisbury, past the general store and the field of dancing statues, and drove on until I came to Zee's driveway.

Her little Jeep was parked in front of her house. I parked beside it, rubbed my sore back, took a deep breath, and walked to the front door.

A little woman wearing a yellow summer dress

opened it to my knock. I looked down at her.

"You must be Zee's sister," I said. "I was expecting her mother."

She beamed and put out a tiny hand. "I'm Maria, and I am her mother. And you must be Jefferson. Please come in."

She led me into the living room. Oliver Underfoot and Velcro came galloping into the room and immediately tangled themselves with my feet, buzzing. Zee came from the kitchen with a smile on her face. "I heard that opening ploy, Jefferson. Very politic. Good grief, what happened to your face?"

"A rhinoceros tried to run over me. I made them take him back to Africa."

She put up a gentle hand and turned my head so she could look at my bruises. She was ever a healer. "No, really, what happened to you?" She stood on her toes and kissed me.

"Actually, it was a barroom brawl. I didn't want to admit it, because I wanted to make a good impression on your mother. I want you to know that it's your fault if she gets the wrong impression of me."

"Thanks a lot. Maybe it would be better if she did get the wrong impression. If she got the right impression, she might try to call off the wedding." She looked down at her mother. "Which story do you prefer? The rhinoceros or the barroom brawl? I'll leave the choice up to you."

"I've never seen either one," said her mother. "I guess I'll take the rhinoceros story, if I have to choose." She peered up at me. "On the other hand, once, when I was a girl, your father and a rival for my affections got into a fight and both of them ended up looking something like this young man looks. So maybe the barroom brawl is a better guess."

Her voice still held the accents of the Azores. She was barely five feet tall, and looked no older than her daughter. I had only been half larking when I'd identified her as Zee's sister. She was obviously one of those people who never age as fast as the rest of us.

"I usually run from violence," I said. "But this time it snuck up on me from behind." I put on my best smile. "They say that if you want to know what a woman will look like in twenty years, you should look at her mother. Zee is the most beautiful woman I know, but I can see that the best is yet to come."

"You are a very shameless fellow," said Maria, blushing slightly. "Such a wicked flatterer probably shouldn't be trusted, but I can see why my daughter has been charmed. Sit down and let me get you something to drink. I believe Zeolinda says you like beer."

"That'll be fine."

I sat, and she went into the kitchen. Zee arched a fine brow and shook her head. "You *are* shameless, Jefferson!" Then she grinned and lowered her voice. "But it's working!"

The people who say flattery will get you nowhere couldn't be more wrong. When Maria Muleto came back with my beer and a glass of wine for herself, I was beginning to relax.

"Now tell me about yourself," she said. "Since my daughter is set upon marrying you, I want to know everything." She sat down on Zee's couch and curled her legs under her, like a young girl.

"I imagine that Zee has told you just about everything."

"She says you're retired. You look very young to be retired."

"I'm only partly retired. I do some fishing to help eke things out."

"She tells me that you were a policeman in Boston, but that you were wounded and left the force."

"That was a long time ago."

"She tells me that you were once married."

"That was before I left the police force. Police wives never know whether their husbands are going to come home. They worry a lot. When I got shot, it was the last straw. My wife stayed with me until I was better, then divorced me. Later, she married a man who had a safer job."

"And then you retired."

"I had some disability money, so I came down here and became a fisherman."

"Zeolinda was married to a doctor. Paul Madieras. I'm sure she's told you about him." Something had changed in her tone. Zee had once told me that her mother had loved having a daughter married to a doctor and had never forgiven her for the divorce.

"We don't talk about him very much," I said. "I'm told he left her for a younger woman after Zee put him through medical school. It's an oft-told story."

Her voice was cool. "He preferred a woman who could appreciate him. Zeolinda isn't always easy to get along with."

I felt a flicker of anger. "Anybody who can't get along with Zee is a fool. When I think of that ex of hers at all, I think of him as Dr. Jerk."

Maria's dark eyes blazed and she looked down at her wine. Well done, J. W. Diplomatic as always.

Maria looked up. "I love my daughter," she said in a tight voice. "I want her to be happy, but I also want her to have some financial security. I want her to be able to stay home with her children, and not have to work when they are young, the way I had to. A woman should be in the home when her children are young."

I did not point out that her daughter had turned out very well in spite of the fact that both of her parents worked. Was Maria comparing my meager money with Dr. Jerk's income? Could be.

"And there is the Church," she went on. "I don't know about your religion, Jefferson, but we are Catholic, so there is the matter of who shall perform the marriage, and how the children will be trained religiously. I know you may think I'm interfering where I have no business to be, and I know that you young people may think that I'm completely old-fashioned and out of date, but this is important. When Zeolinda and Paul separated, there was an annulment, so both were free to remarry. Was your marriage annulled as well? I want Zeolinda's marriage to be completely proper. You understand."

I thought I understood very well indeed. We were in a mire, and there seemed no likely way out. I tried to keep my voice level, but didn't think I managed it. "My first wife and I were not married in the Catholic Church, so we needed no annulment when we were divorced. Zee and I are getting married in the yard outside John Skye's farmhouse. I think it will be quite a proper marriage. My sister and our friends will be there to help us celebrate. I want you and your family to be there, too. Zee has chosen a friend of hers to marry us. I believe she's a justice of the peace. As for the children we may have, my sister, who lives in Santa Fe, New Mexico, is not a Catholic, but sends her children to a Catholic school because it's the best school she can find. That makes sense to me. Should Zee and I have children, and I hope we do, I plan to send them to the best schools we can afford. If they're Catholic schools, that's fine. If they're not, that's fine, too. If Zee wants to raise our children as Catholics, that's okay with me, although they'll have to get used to living with a father who isn't one."

She drank some of her wine and sat stiffly in her chair. "You are not a religious man, then?"

I said, "I think religions are metaphors for spiritual truth. Maybe that makes me religious." If I'd stopped there, it might have been okay, but because I am by nature occasionally perverse and self-destructive, I kept talking. "Personally, I usually don't go to church unless there's music that I want to hear. Like it says in *Ivanhoe*, 'the closer to church, the farther from God.' "

She got up. "I'd better help Zeolinda in the kitchen," she said, and walked out of the room.

▪ 18 ▪

"How'd it go?" asked Quinn the next morning. I looked at him across the breakfast table. He looked back. "I withdraw the question," he said, and returned his attention to his blueberry pancakes.

"That bad, eh?" asked Dave.

I wasn't sure whether it had been that bad or not. I was sure that it hadn't been good. Maria and I had been very polite all through supper, and afterward I'd left early.

"I invited them here for supper tonight," I said.

"Ah," nodded Quinn. "The old home court advantage. Good thinking, Ace."

"Too bad you don't have a piano," said Dave. "I could play background music. Something Portuguese and soothing."

Quinn looked at him. "Aha. That's the first time I've heard you mention a piano since we got down here. I do believe that you have taken the cure and are about ready to return to the concert world or whatever it is you call that life you live."

Dave gave a little nod. "You may be right." He held up his right hand and flexed his fingers. "I think that after about one more trip to the fishing grounds I'll be ready to face the world with a smile."

"We can do that," I said.

"Sorry," said Quinn. "You can't come. You have to

clean up this house and do the cooking for your guests. Dave and I will have to face the bluefish alone."

I hated to admit it, but he had a point.

"You know, you just might help me out a little," I said. "Vacuum the place, pick up your junk. That sort of thing."

"You sound just like my ex-wife," said Quinn. "Sorry, but Dave and I are guests, so we don't have to do any work. We're just down here to loaf. Come on, Dave, my boy, we're off to Wasque."

Dave hesitated. I turned my back on Quinn and winked at Dave. "Go on," I said. "If you stay, Quinn will stay too, and I'll have to listen to him moan and groan while I trip all over him. If he's around, it'll take me twice as long to get things done." I dug the Toyota keys out of my pocket and tossed them to him. "Bring home a bluefish for supper."

"Well . . ."

"You heard him," said Quinn. "Let's get out of here before he changes his mind."

"Just leave your car keys," I said. "I might have to go somewhere."

"No farther than the liquor store, I hope," said Quinn, handing me his keys. "Try to buy a decent wine, for a change."

When they were gone, I started some bread—since what is more winning than fresh, homemade bread?—then dragged out the vacuum cleaner (salvaged almost new from the dump years before, needing only a cord which I got from another vacuum cleaner otherwise quite worthless). While it was still in the cool of the morning, I vacuumed the whole house, then picked up bachelor-abandoned beer cans, magazines, newspapers, and other clutter, and tidied up in general. Dave was pretty neat, but Quinn was not. He tended to live very informally, except for his car and his clothes, both of which he tended with great care.

"Image is everything," he liked to say.

"What about women?" I'd asked him once. "How do

you keep the pristine image intact when you live like a pig?"

"The secret is never to entertain at home," he'd replied. "We go to their places, if we go anywhere. They love a mystery, and my apartment makes me one. They want to see it, and the more I don't let them, the more fascinating I become. Works like a charm. Of course some of their places are as sloppy as mine, or worse, but what the hell?"

Indeed. I didn't think of myself as a real neatnik, but compared to Quinn I was tidy to a fault, which only meant that I liked things more or less in order, or at least stacked in orderly piles.

While I worked, I wondered not for the first time why we pick up our houses when we know we're going to have visitors, even though the visitors must know the houses don't look like that most of the time. Vanity of some kind, apparently: we want to be thought of as better than we really are. We want to make a good impression. Or, to put a better spin on it, maybe we want to honor our guests by cleaning up for them.

When I thought the house was clean enough, I punched down the bread. I punch mine down four times, since it seems to improve the grain of the finished product. It was still only mid-morning, so I called Hazel Fine at the Vineyard Haven National Bank.

"Perfect timing," she said. "I was about to call you. I talked to a pal over at the Zimmerman National Bank in Hyannis, and he's interested in this business. No banker wants his firm to get involved in a scam, even if everything his own bank has done is completely legal and aboveboard. Another thing: it turns out my friend knows some people over at Frazier Information Systems, so he's going to try to talk to them. He's also going to try to track down the New Bedford, Woods Hole and Nantucket Salvage Company."

"Sounds like he's going to be a busy guy. Will he talk to me after he does all of his checking?"

"Bankers aren't too quick to discuss their business

with people they don't know. Especially people without any authority to be asking questions."

"A perfect description of me."

"Among other descriptions I've heard."

"Everybody's a wise guy. I didn't even snicker when you rattled off that bit about honest bankers and didn't even mention the S and L guys, and now you give me the stick. Jeez . . ."

"Goodness me. I'd forgotten how sensitive you are, Jefferson. I can't begin to tell you how sorry I am for hurting your feelings. How can I possibly hope to make amends?"

"I'm afraid it may be too late for that."

"I'm thinking of taking tomorrow off and catching the Hy-line over to the Cape. How about coming along with me? We can talk to my man over there and, with luck, maybe see some people at FIS, too. Maybe we can even find the salvage company. Perhaps we might actually locate Cecil Jones or Glen Gordon. What do you say? The boat leaves Oak Bluffs just after eleven and we can be back on the island by seven-thirty."

"I say I'll make a phone call and rent a car over there. We'll need wheels."

"No problem. My friend will pick us up at the boat, give us his car for the day, and take us back to the boat when we leave."

"What a guy. And people say that bankers are all a bunch of tight-fisted, fishy-eyed, cold-hearted thieves who wouldn't help a blind child across the street unless they get paid for it."

"They say that, do they? Damn! They've found us out! I knew we were wasting our money on those PR firms! I'll meet you at the Hy-line dock tomorrow, then."

"I'll be wearing a red rose in my hair, so you'll recognize me."

I rang off, and glanced at my watch. If Beth Goodwin's schedule was the same as the last time I'd visited her, she'd still be at home. I got into the Toyota and drove to her place. As I stopped in front of the farmhouse Peter

Dennison came out of the front door. He looked puzzled, then recognized me and came over to the truck.

"Hi," he said. "Beth said you came by yesterday." He was wearing a white tee shirt and dark pants. Kitchen clothes for the afternoon shift at the restaurant where he worked, I guessed.

"I wondered if you happen to have a picture of Glen Gordon, Kathy's boyfriend."

He leaned a bony arm on the door. "I don't think so. Kathy's folks came by a couple of days ago and took all of her stuff. If she had a picture of him, it's not here now."

"I'm going over to the Cape tomorrow. I thought I might try to talk to him. What does he look like?"

He frowned the way people do when you ask them impossible questions like "How did it taste?," "What does he look like?," and so forth. But also like most of those people, he gave it a shot: "I don't know. Let's see: shorter than me. A little under six feet, maybe. Sort of brownish hair, sort of average build, not skinny like me, but not fat either, you know what I mean. Lemme see . . . I don't remember his eyes. He's clean-shaven . . . That's about it. Sort of a normal-looking guy."

The normal-looking guys are the worst kind to describe. If Glen Gordon had been seven feet tall, or if he'd had tattoos all over his face, Peter Dennison could have described him to a T. Oh well.

"Say," said Peter, "that's Denise, isn't it? Nice picture."

I followed his gaze down to the photograph of Denise Vale that lay on the passenger seat, where I'd left it so I wouldn't forget to return it to her father.

"You know her?" I asked.

"Well, not really. I saw her up here a couple of times. She was a friend of Kathy's. That's how I met her. Funny girl."

"A friend of Kathy's, you say."

"Yeah. I think they met at school in some play Kathy was in. She used to come up here to see Kathy."

"What about?"

"Hey, don't ask me. They usually talked in Kathy's room. I only saw her coming or going."

"They met at NYU, you say."

"I think so. I never really asked and they never really said, but I got that idea somehow. Maybe Beth knows." He glanced at the watch on his thin wrist. "Hey, I got to get to work. Nice seeing you again."

He walked around the corner of the house and came back with a bicycle upon which he immediately pedaled away. I looked after him, thinking, then went up to the door and knocked. No answer. I walked around to the back of the house, whistling the drinking song from *La Traviata*, so as not to surprise Beth in case she was sunbathing nude in the backyard. I sometimes work on my all-over tan in my own yard, so I knew how pleasant the experience could be. Personally, I never cared if I was surprised or not, but people have different ideas about such things.

Beth was there, wearing the same tiny bathing suit as yesterday. Apparently that was as near to naked sunning as she cared to come, which was pretty close, at that. She pushed up her dark glasses and smiled at me.

"Caught loafing once again. You must think this is all I do."

"It looks okay to me." I gestured over my shoulder with my thumb. "I just saw your friend Peter. He told me that a girl named Denise Vale used to come here to see Kathy. Is that right?"

"Yeah." She frowned. "Why do you ask?"

"Her father is looking for her. I thought you might know where he could look."

She slid the glasses back over her eyes and sank back down on her lounge chair. "She lives somewhere in Oak Bluffs, I think. I don't really know her."

Both her tone and her action said more than her words. Beth didn't like Denise Vale.

"Peter called her a funny girl," I said. "What do you think he meant?"

She shrugged. "I don't think 'funny' is the word I'd use."

"What word would you use?"

"I don't know. Bitchy? Cold?"

"How so?"

Again, the shrug. "Kathy was always sort of down after Denise's visits. And Denise never was what you'd call warm to Peter and me."

"Peter said Denise and Kathy were friends."

"They knew each other and Denise came up here every now and then, but I don't know if that made them friends. A friend is somebody who makes you happy. I never saw Denise make Kathy happy."

I thought that was a pretty good definition. "What did they talk about?"

"I asked Kathy that once, after Denise went home. She said they just talked. You know, the stuff everybody talks about. Guys, work, school, that sort of thing."

"Did they meet at NYU? I know they both went there."

"Yeah, I think maybe they did. Denise was a couple of years ahead of Kathy. Say, do you mind if we talk about something else? I'm getting depressed."

Life is suffering, as the Buddha said.

"One more thing before I leave you and old Sol alone together. Do you have a picture of Glen Gordon? I'd like to know what he looks like."

"No. All Kathy's stuff is gone." Then she thought of something. "Say, I think I have a snap of him and Kathy together. The last time he was here before she died. It's still in my camera."

I dug out some money. "Look, if you'll take the roll out of the camera, I'll pay you to get it developed and buy you a new film to replace it. I'd really like to see what Gordon looks like."

"Why do you want to know that?"

I told her what I'd told Peter Dennison, and that seemed to satisfy her. "I'm going over to the Cape tomorrow morning," I added. "If you can get that picture developed by mid-morning, I'll pick it up before I go."

She took my money and I went home and punched down the bread again. With the fresh bread and a salad, I was serving coquilles St. Jacques for supper, and that wouldn't take long to prepare, but I wanted to start off with littlenecks on the half shell and clams casino, which meant that I had to go quahogging.

I got my rake and my small wire basket and headed for Katama Bay, where the littlenecks and cherrystones live. While I was raking, I could try to do some clear thinking. It seemed to me that I could stand to do a bit of that, for a change. One thing was certain: I had plenty of subject matter.

■ 19 ■

I t took me an hour to get the littlenecks and cherry-stones I needed, which was about the right amount of time since I had to go home then and give the bread its third punching. South of me, along the beach, there were dozens of four-wheel-drive vehicles, and the air was full of kites. The June People were down, working on the tans they planned to take home with them. There were blankets and umbrellas and coolers and gas grills, and balls and Frisbees sailed back and forth. A good time was being had by all, and not one person there was concerned about Kathy Ellis, Denise Vale, Maria Muleto, or any of the other people I had been thinking about. Maybe they were all smarter than I.

Quahogging involves wading out into shallow water with a floating basket tied to your waist, and scratching around on the bottom with a quahog rake. When you find a quahog, it feels and sounds something like, but not quite like, hitting a rock. After a while you know a quahog when you've found one, and you no longer get excited about hitting rocks. Conchs and the occasional horseshoe crab, however, often feel like quahogs and serve to make the game seem a bit chancier than it would otherwise be.

Quahogs are hard-shell clams that are true gifts from the sea. The smallest keepers are littlenecks, which are usually eaten raw on the half shell and which cost a shocking amount if you buy them in downtown Edgartown, considering how easy they are to catch. Cherrystones are the next step up, and I use them mostly for clams casino—clams on the half shell, topped by garlic butter, some bread crumbs, and a bit of bacon, and broiled until the bacon is done. Delish! Even people who say they don't like clams like casinos, and no wonder. You can also french fry the little guys if you want to, and I often do. The bigger quahogs usually become stuffers or find their way into chowders. You can make a lot of different kinds of meals out of quahogs, and all of them are good.

Quahogging does not require much concentrated thought, so while your hands are raking you can send your brain off on business of its own. Alone out there in the water, while I scratched away, I sent mine back to that day when Zee had discovered an extra hundred thousand dollars in her checking account, then had it follow the pattern of incidents that seemed tied to that event. Because Kathy Ellis had happened to die in my driveway, I had gotten involved, whereas I'd not otherwise have done so. But now I didn't expect to get uninvolved until I either knew what was going on or I decided that I was never going to know. Whatever was happening involved some pretty big money and maybe murder, too. The money was only a curiosity to me, since money is too mysterious for me to take it seriously, but if someone had killed Kathy Ellis, I'd take that very personally.

And of course all of this was happening when I should have been thinking more than anything else of my wedding, for God's sake. In less than three weeks I was going to get married, and so far all I'd really managed to contribute to the celebration was to get the *Shirley J.* ready for the scheduled honeymoon trip to Nantucket and to alienate Zee's mother. What a romantic devil I was turning out to be.

But if tonight's meal went right, my relations with my potential mother-in-law might improve. The way to the heart is through the belly, they say, whoever they may be. Zee, although slender and sleek as an otter, had an appetite like a horse. Maybe Maria was just as much an eater. If so, there was hope of regaining lost ground.

When I had enough quahogs, I drove home and punched down the bread again. Then I had a cold bottle of Sam Adams and a ham and avocado sandwich, and went, basket on my arm, out to the garden to pick the salad stuff I'd need. Since the Vineyard's mild climate allows for early garden planting, I had plenty of good things growing. If Maria didn't like this salad, there was something wrong with her.

Back inside, I rinsed and dried the veggies and made up a honey-mustard dressing. I put everything in the fridge, got another beer, and went to work on the St. Jacques. Some of the nice things about coquilles St. Jacques are that it's delicious, it's pretty easy to make, and it can be prepared ahead of time. The secret of its flavor is, of course, butter and cream, the magic ingredients in a lot of French sauces, and a couple I use in spite of our current national case of cholesterolphobia.

You can make St. Jacques with any kind or combination of white fish or shrimp, but since I still had a goodly supply of frozen scallops from last winter, I used those. I boiled mushrooms, butter, white wine, and onion, with thyme, a bay leaf, and some lemon juice, and then added the scallops and let the whole thing simmer for a couple of more minutes. Then I stirred up a sauce out of flour, more butter, juice from the drained scallops, egg yolks, some heavy cream, and just enough salt and pepper. When the sauce began to coat my stirring spoon, I put the scallop mixture in a casserole, and spooned the sauce over it, extracting the bay leaf en route. A mixture of bread crumbs and grated Parmesan over the top, and a dribble of melted butter over that and, *voilà!*

I put the St. Jacques in the fridge beside the salad, and made four loaves of bread and set them to rise.

Good work, J. W. I had another Sam Adams and set the table for five, using my best almost matching flatware and china. A classy meal deserved a classy setting. With luck, Maria would be so captivated by the food and company that she'd forget about religion. A consummation devoutly to be wished.

I heard the Land Cruiser coming down the driveway, and went out to meet Dave and Quinn. They were happy. And no wonder: there were a dozen nice seven- or eight-pound blues in the fish box.

"We're going to smoke these guys," grinned Dave. "They'll love 'em up in Boston. I'm going to eat smoked bluefish every day as long as my supply lasts."

"So you're heading back?" I said.

"The master musician has risen from the dead," said Quinn. "It's time to return to the mortal world."

"How much trouble are you going to be in?" I asked Dave.

He shrugged. "Some people will be pissed off, but that's why I have a manager. I pay him a lot of money to handle problems, and he's good at it." A wry look appeared on his face. "I will admit, though, that I never did anything like this to him before."

"Maybe it's a good precedent," I said. "Maybe people will get used to the notion that every now and then you need to disappear for some R and R."

"Yeah," said Quinn, nodding. "The right PR and it could become part of your professional mystique. You know: brooding pianist famous for unexplained disappearances. We could take some sort of shadowy photographs of you in unidentified places and slip them to the papers. I think you might get a lot of mileage out of it."

"What I want to get right now is a bunch of fillets from these fish," said Dave.

"You know where the filleting table is," I said. "I'll get you a couple of knives. One of the rules about fish is: if you catch 'em, you clean 'em."

"That sounds like a rule you just made up," said Quinn, taking one handle of the fish box while Dave took the other. They went off to the table behind my shed, and I went through the house and collected two filleting knives. At the table I watched the two of them work on the fish until I was sure that Dave wouldn't cut off one of his valuable fingers, then went back into the house and filled a pan with water and the salt and sugar combination that I use to soak fish in overnight before smoking them.

When Dave and Quinn brought in the fillets, we put them in the water and found a place for the pan in the fridge, which by then was getting pretty full.

While Quinn was showering, I got a surprise from Dave. He went out to the Land Cruiser and came back with an electric keyboard.

"Look at this," he said. "We found this in the thrift shop downtown on our way home. It may not be a Steinway, but you can play it." He took it into the living room, plugged it in, and ran his fingers over the keys. The room filled with music. "I need practice," said Dave, flexing his fingers. "My surf-casting muscles are getting better, but my piano playing ones are out of shape." Again, he touched the keys and again the room was filled with better music than anyone had previously made there. "Well, what do you think?" he asked. "Not bad, eh?"

"Not bad at all."

"Now here's what I have in mind. Music hath charms to soothe the savage breast . . . or is it savage beast? I can never remember . . . Anyway, I thought that if I contributed some background music or maybe even a little pre- or post-dinner entertainment, maybe Zee's mom might cool her fires a little. What do you think?"

"You know any soothe-the-Portuguese-mother-in-law-to-be music?"

"Leave it to me. I can probably come up with a few tunes that'll do the job."

"Maybe some of those moon songs. *Clair de Lune* and the *Moonlight Sonata*, and like that."

"Yeah," said Dave. "That's the idea. Or maybe I'll serve up some fados. Just leave it to me."

Quinn came in, wrapped in his towel, and Dave headed for the shower. "Don't worry," said Quinn. "I know this is a big night for you, so I'm going to put on a clean shirt and I won't spit on the floor."

Things didn't look too bad. Good food, good drink, Quinn, who, if he wished, could charm the ladies, and the world's champion pianist to provide entertainment. I went into the kitchen to attend to the final details: first, the bread. I put it in the oven. If all else failed, the smell of fresh cooked bread should win Maria's heart.

While the loaves baked, I opened the littlenecks and cherrystones and prepared the casinos. I finished just as the bread was done. Perfect timing.

Quinn, Dave, and I ate most of a loaf as soon as the bread was out of the oven. We cut thick slices and slathered them with butter, and wolfed them down. Yum! We had some more, and washed them down with beer.

"How many of those have you had?" asked Quinn, looking at my Sam Adams. "You don't want Maria to think you're a boozer."

"Just the right number," I said. I felt good.

I brushed my teeth one last time, and slid into another shirt. In the mirror I looked as passable as I ever get. I put martini glasses in the freezer to chill, and looked at my watch. Waiting time. I noticed that I was nervous.

Right on schedule, Zee's little Jeep came down my driveway. Dave and Quinn, decked out even more nicely than I was, went out with me to greet Zee and Maria.

Quinn and I got kisses from Zee. Then I introduced Maria to Quinn.

"Just Quinn?" she asked with a little smile. "No first name? Like in *Shane*?"

"I always thought Shane was his first name," said Quinn. "Quinn is a last name, like Spenser."

"I always thought Spenser was his first name," said Dave. "That's what inspired me to be only Dave." He gave Maria a small bow. "Hi," he said. "I'm Dave."

"No you're not," she said, pointing a finger at him. "I

know who you are. You're David Greenstein. Zeolinda gave me a tape of yours and there was a picture of you on the case. Besides, your face has been all over the Boston papers. You're a missing person!"

He spread his hands. "Not for long, I'm afraid. I'm headed back to civilization in a couple of days. Then it's back to work."

Maria studied him approvingly, and I saw some deviltry in her eye. "You are a wonderful pianist. Are you married?"

Dave looked surprised. "No, I'm afraid not."

Maria turned to Zee. "There you are, dear. Another eligible man. Jefferson isn't the only one left, after all, in spite of what you've been telling me."

"Mom!" said Zee.

"What do you say, David?" asked Maria. "My daughter here wants to get married. Are you interested?"

"Gosh, Zee," said Dave. "This is so sudden."

"She's a great find, Dave," I said. "Beautiful, a steady job, has a sweetheart of a mother. You could do a lot worse."

Zee tugged at my hand. "You *do* have my triple vodka martini waiting for me inside, of course."

"This may be your last chance, Dave," said Maria. "Once he wraps that martini around her, I'm afraid she'll never be able to leave him."

"Actually," said Dave, running his eyes over her from face to foot and back again, "I've always been attracted to more mature women. Let me see your left hand. Rats. Still married, I see. Is there any chance of winning you away from whoever it is who has you now?"

"You don't want to marry a musician," said Quinn, stepping in. "I know he seems like a romantic figure, but he's away in some foreign country most of the time, being chased by dark-eyed beauties such as yourself. What you want is an honest, hard-working member of the fourth estate like me. I'm adoring and absolutely dependable, exactly the kind of man you really need. I'd like the two of us to get off to a proper start, so what can I get you to drink?"

"White wine," said Maria, flicking her dark eyes at first one of the men and then the other.

Dave took her arm. "You get the drinks," he said to Quinn. "I'll escort Maria up to the balcony. Come along, madam. We'll let the servants attend us."

"I think this evening may work out all right," whispered Zee, her smile flashing.

And it did. At the end of the evening, after the drinks and the food and the music and the talk, I got my first kiss from Maria as she and Zee were leaving for home. When they were gone, I poured three last glasses of cognac, and Dave, Quinn, and I sat in the living room. Dave was back to the keyboard and let his hands run over the instrument. Some gentle air I'd never heard. It sounded just right.

"Background music," said Quinn, sipping his drink. "Too bad we can't have it all the time. Did I ever tell you my theory that the trouble with life is that there's no background music?"

"You mean the one about walking past some girl and not realizing that it's a potentially romantic situation because there aren't any violins playing, or not realizing that you're about to get mugged because there's no ominous music?"

"Yeah. Well, did I ever tell you about my theory that the trouble with life is that there's no plot?"

"Is that like the telephone directory theory? That it has a tremendous cast, but no script?"

"It's nice to know that at least you've been listening," said Quinn.

Dave looked up from his keyboard. He smiled. "I saw that kiss from Maria," he said. "Louis, I think this is the beginning of a beautiful friendship."

▪ 20 ▪

I was up early to get started on smoking Dave's and Quinn's fish. I rinsed them to wash off whatever salt was on the surface of the fillets, then I set them to air-dry for an hour on racks. After that, I put the racks in the smoker that sits out behind my shed, beside the filleting table.

My smoker is an old metal refrigerator salvaged from the town dump in the good old days before the environmentalists seized control of it and banished dump picking from the list of approved island activities, and I heat my hickory chips with an electric stove-top unit found, where else, in the dump of the golden age.

I put the chips in an old cast-iron skillet (found guess where), put the skillet on the heating unit, and turned on just enough juice to smolder the chips. By that time, Dave and Quinn were up, and I told them how to keep the smoke roiling until the fish were done.

"You should be done about noon," I said. "Then take the racks out and let the fillets cool. Then take the skins off, wrap them in plastic wrap, and stick them in the fridge."

"After sampling them to make sure they're okay, of course," said Dave.

"Of course." Quinn nodded. "And we should still have time to hit the beach for a couple of hours in the afternoon. Ah, the Vineyard life." He looked at Dave.

"What do you think? Should we move down here permanently? You could probably get a job playing in a bar, and I could maybe go to work at the *Gazette* or the *Times*."

Dave arched a brow. "And I could woo Zee while I was here. That would probably make Maria very happy. This idea deserves some thought."

"Maybe you could woo Maria, too, while you're at it," said Quinn.

"Good-bye, you bozos," I said.

I climbed into Quinn's car and drove to the farmhouse where Beth Goodwin and Peter Dennison lived. Beth still had sleepy eyes when she came to the door. She hadn't even been to the photo place to see if her film was ready. So things go. "I'll come back tomorrow, just before noon," I said, and drove on to Oak Bluffs.

The Hy-line passenger ferries run between Oak Bluffs and Hyannis, and between Oak Bluffs and Nantucket. The *Island Queen*, another passenger ferry, runs between Oak Bluffs and Falmouth. Between them, they haul a lot of day tourists back and forth, and keep Oak Bluffs harbor pretty busy.

I parked the car over on the beach side of the parking lot. I was early, so I sat and watched the harbor traffic. Oak Bluffs has a very small harbor, but there are usually interesting boats there, and like many other people, I never get tired of looking at boats and the sea. Today I particularly admired a nice little folkboat that sailed out of the harbor on a following wind. Several folkboats have crossed the Atlantic and at least one was sailed around the world single-handed by a woman who had a lot more skill and courage than I have. There's something in human beings that draws them to water. They build houses beside streams, rivers, lakes, and the sea. They like to look at water, wade in it, fish in it, swim in it. They like the way it sounds, and the way its appearance changes with the weather. They even like its fearful power, when flood or storm changes it into a great destroyer. They like to float leaves on it, and to make toy and real boats, and to build bridges over it. It fascinates them and that fascination never leaves them. No wonder that in the Koran, paradise is often described as a garden where lovely waters flow.

"You are looking quite philosophical," said Helen Fine, sitting down beside me.

"Boats," I said. "Just messing around with boats. There's nothing like it, nothing at all."

"Rat said something like that, as I recall."

"I only know enough to misquote. You're early."

"Not too early. There, I believe, is our boat."

True. We watched the Hy-line ferry grow larger as it churned toward us across Nantucket Sound. It came into harbor between the stone jetties, turned and made fast to its dock. Tourists wearing dark glasses and loaded with cameras and bags streamed off, and when they were all ashore, we and the other mainland-bound passengers went aboard. At eleven-fifteen, we were cast off and on our way.

With only a gentle following wind to stir up the waves, we had a fast, smooth passage across the sound, and were soon tying up at Hyannis, which is famous for its Kennedys, among other things. In spite of its many attributes, Hyannis is not my favorite place. Too many people in too small a place. I wondered how long it would take Edgartown to get that way.

More people had been going from the mainland to the island than from the island to the mainland, so there weren't many of us to unload. The opposite condition would prevail on the evening boat, when the Vineyard day trippers came back to America and a few islanders headed back for home.

We walked ashore at one, and a youngish-looking guy wearing a summer suit met us. Helen did the honors.

"Matthew, this is J. W. Jackson; J. W., this is Matt Jung."

"Jung as in famous psychiatrist," said Matt, "but I am a mere banker." His hands were very clean, but his grip was firm. "Have you had lunch? No? Well, let's do that.

We can talk and eat at the same time. I'm starving."

There was a café not far from the dock, and we found a table in spite of the noon crowd. It took awhile for us to get sandwiches, beers for the guys, and white wine for Helen, but we didn't waste the time.

Matt Jung looked at me without unfriendliness, but without friendliness either. "Helen's told me about your interest in this business. She says you're a man who can be trusted."

"Not to add two and two and get four every time. That's another reason why I'm not a banker. Balance is a word unknown to my checkbook."

"I wasn't thinking about your abilities as a mathematician."

"I'm just telling you that I can't always be trusted to be too bright. Still, you may have some information that will help us get to the bottom of whatever it is that's going on. If you do, we'd like to have it. If you're wondering whether you can trust me with it, maybe I should leave so you can talk to Helen alone. I don't mind doing that."

He pursed his lips. "And later you can get it from Helen."

"If she wants to give it to me. I don't plan on beating it out of her with a rubber hose."

Helen gave him her winning smile. "J. W. is just a little touchy because he's hungry, dear. He'll be much nicer when he gets his beer. I assure you that you can tell him anything you can tell me."

I looked at her. "Touchy? Me, touchy till I get my beer?"

She patted my hand. "There, there, J. W. You probably just never noticed it. Who was it that said we are three people: the one we think we are, the one other people think we are, and the one we really are?"

"Pogo?"

"A Pogo fan, eh?" Matt Jung seemed to brighten, though he still looked neither unfriendly nor friendly. "The old Pogo or the new Pogo?"

"The old Pogo, of course. I inherited my father's collection of Pogo books—*Pogo, I Go Pogo, The Pogo Papers*, and all the rest."

Matt leaned forward. "This is a test," he said. "If you pass, I'll reveal all, since a true Pogo fan can be trusted with anything. What was the star in the white?"

"Piece of cake: a word of white."

Matt sat back and smiled first at Helen and then at me.

Helen frowned at us both. "What is this? A secret code? Do you both belong to one of those men's organizations or something? One of those clubs named after an animal, with passwords and handshakes?"

" 'The star is a word of white, of white. The star in the wind is a word,' " I explained.

"Exactly." Matt nodded. "Well, what do you folks want to know?"

"Everything you've found out," said Helen. "J. W., I expect a full explanation of this star is a word stuff on the way home."

"It's a literary allusion," I said, looking at my nails.

"It's certainly eluded me." She paused as our drinks and food arrived. "Ah. Now, gentlemen, let us devote our attentions to things I understand: vittles and banking."

My beer and sandwich were not bad. Being smarter than some presidents of the United States, Helen and I could eat and listen at the same time, and Matt Jung could eat and talk.

"After we talked, Helen, I went over our files and found out that, yes, checks from your bank were deposited in our bank, in the account of the New Bedford, Woods Hole and Nantucket Salvage Company. The company address, by the way, is a P.O. box in Falmouth. The guy who opened the account is Cecil Jones, the company treasurer. He and his assistant, a woman named Marilyn Grimes, are authorized to make withdrawals. The account was opened in April with a five-hundred-dollar deposit, then stayed quiet until early June, when it began to get deposits mostly in nine-thousand-dollar amounts. Last week, though, it got a deposit of one hundred thousand dollars.

"Since we're required by law to report any transactions of ten thousand dollars or more to the government, we reported that last deposit."

"But not the smaller ones?" asked Helen.

"No, because there wasn't any reason to be suspicious of them. A deposit or a withdrawal of several thousand dollars by a corporation is not unusual, as you know." Matt paused to wash down some sandwich with some beer. "Now here's something more interesting. We've got bank branches in three other places on the Cape: Sandwich, Chatham, and Provincetown. About two weeks ago, the New Bedford, Woods Hole and Nantucket Salvage Company started making withdrawals from their account. The withdrawals were from the various branches of the bank, and sometimes were made on the same day. They were always for several thousand dollars—pretty close to nine thousand dollars one way or the other, and always for cash. But since there was always enough money to cover the withdrawals, and Cecil Jones or his assistant never made more than one at any branch of the bank in a given week, they never attracted anybody's attention. In fact, if you hadn't called me, Helen, we still wouldn't have any reason to pay any attention to the transactions."

"They may be innocent as doves," said Helen.

"Could be," agreed Matt.

"How much money is still in the company account?" I asked.

"Of course that's confidential information," said Matt. "But since you know that the star is a word, I'll tell you. About a thou over one hundred thousand dollars."

"And there was about a hundred thousand in the account before last week's big hundred-thousand-dollar deposit . . ."

"Correct. Which means that the hundred thousand that was deposited earlier has now been withdrawn."

"As cash."

Matt nodded. "As cash."

"And where did it go?"

"Who knows? To pay expenses for the New Bedford, Woods Hole and Nantucket Salvage Company, presumably."

"Do you know many corporations that pay their bills in cash?"

Matt finished off his sandwich. "Not one."

"Laundered money," said Helen, sipping her wine. "On the other hand, there's nothing illegal about paying debts in cash."

"Nothing at all," agreed Matt.

"Unusual, though."

"What about the hundred thou that's still in the account?" I asked.

"What about it?"

"It sounds to me like Cecil is pretty apt to make a big cash withdrawal pretty soon."

Matt shrugged. "It's his company's money. He can take it out whenever he wants to."

"Do you have a picture of Cecil?"

"Better than that, I have him on video. We keep cameras going at all of our branches and they record all business transactions. A security precaution, in case somebody sticks up the joint. It'll take me some time to go through the film, but since we know when and where deposits and withdrawals were made, we can correlate those places and times with the film we have."

"How soon do you think you can come up with a video?"

"Video is not my specialty. Tomorrow? Later today, maybe? I'll have to find somebody who knows more about video than I do."

"Don't look at me," I said. "I don't even have a TV."

Helen finished her wine. "What have you found out about Frazier Information Systems?"

"Perfectly respectable firm. Branches all over the Northeast. New England, New York, Pennsylvania, New

Jersey. Good reputation. You should know, Helen. Your bank has been doing business with them."

"Yes, I know. Did you find out anything about the man named Glen Gordon?"

Matt reached into an inside pocket and pulled out a small notebook. He thumbed through the pages until he found the one he sought. "Glen Gordon," he read. "Twenty-six, graduate of NYU, BA in math and computers, been with FIS for five years, reputation of being a hard worker, likes beach days off in the summer, so sometimes works clear through the night to get the free day time, single, but has girlfriends, well liked and competent." Matt looked up from the notebook. "I got that from a secretary and again from one of the VP's. They both agree that Glen Gordon is just the kind of guy you'd want working for you. That work all night for a day off is the only thing that even looks half unusual, and even that works out well for the company because Gordon gets a lot done when he works alone."

I looked at Helen. "Clotho is spinning her web," I said.

"First, the star is a word, and now Clotho is spinning her web." She shook her head. "Everything's a mystery. I must have been culturally deprived as a child."

▪ 21 ▪

"The star in the wind is an image in a Walt Kelly poem," said Matt.

"And Clotho is one of the fates," I said. "The one who spins the thread of our destiny before Lachesis measures how long it will be and Atropos cuts it off."

"Oh," said Helen. "Illiterate me."

I patted her hand. "It's all a matter of having read *Pogo* and *Classic Comics*. Unlike Matt here, most bankers-to-be don't waste their time on such stuff. They're buried in *The Wall Street Journal* from the time they're in kindergarten. Don't blame yourself."

"Don't worry," said Helen. "I won't." She turned to Matt. "I'd like to talk to somebody at Frazier Information Systems. They're here in town somewhere, aren't they? I've never met her, but in the past I've talked on the phone with a woman named Maple Appleyard."

He nodded. "Their place is just beyond the big traffic circle, going toward Falmouth. My car, such as it is, is at your disposal." He flipped again through his little notebook and tore out a page. "Here's the address. I've talked to Maple, too, by the way." He looked at me. "I know it sounds like a made-up name, but it's real. Her parents gave her the first one, and she got the second one from her husband. She says she only married him so she could have the name. She runs FIS's Hyannis office." He handed Helen a set of keys and pointed at a middle-aged Ford down the street.

"We'll leave the car in the lot behind the bank," said Helen. "I'll lock it and put the keys on top of the left front tire." She gestured to the waitress. "I'll get this bill."

Neither gentleman at the table argued at all.

The big traffic circle is inland from downtown Hyannis. Highways sprout from it in various directions, and along Route 28 toward Falmouth we soon found Frazier Information Services housed in a large wooden building occupied by various businesses.

Inside, a secretary looked at Helen's card, made a call, and waved us into an office. A woman in her thirties, wearing a business suit and shoes with one-inch heels, came to meet us. Her hair was brown and thick, and was tucked up in some sort of bun.

For reasons which elude me, businesswomen seem to think that they have to do severe things with their hair and clothing in order to command respect. I tend to judge people by how they behave and what they say, rather than by how they dress.

On the other hand, even Zee, who is about as independent as they come, knots her hair up and wears a uniform when she's working, and I had worn chopped hair and a uniform while I was in the army and while I was a cop. So maybe I didn't have a case.

Such were my lofty thoughts as we sat down in front of Maple Appleyard's desk, and I tuned into the conversation that had already started.

"I'm afraid that I can't introduce you to Glen Gordon," Maple was saying. "This is one of his beach days. Tomorrow is another one. He earned them by working nights last week. I think he said that there's some sort of a musical bash this coming weekend—a rock concert or some such thing up near Boston—so he's managed to get himself four days off in a row."

"Isn't that a little unusual?" asked Helen.

"We try to be as flexible as we can, as far as scheduling is concerned. Women with small children—men, too, for that matter—can work unconventional hours so they can be home with the kids when they have to be. That sort of thing. We know that life doesn't happen on a schedule. Some people can work eight to five, and others can't. So we let people set their own schedules as much as possible."

"Doesn't that make it difficult for a manager?"

"Maybe. On the other hand, I'm not always here between dawn and dusk myself. Sometimes I put in long shifts and sometimes I'm gone for a day and one of my assistants takes over. The secret is to have good people working for you."

"I'd think your productivity might suffer."

"It doesn't. Or if it does, then we have a talk with whoever isn't pulling his load. Usually we can work out a resolution. We change a shift, we adjust responsibilities, we try different solutions. If it's something we can work out, we work it out. Maybe the person just can't do full-time work here and full-time work at home. We might let him do part-time work until things at home get better, then bring him back full-time. If somebody needs more training, we try to see that he gets it.

"But if we decide that the person just can't do the work, we do what any business would do: we let him go. We're only going to stay in business as long as we can deliver the goods, so they have to be delivered. The biggest difference between us and most other businesses is that we really don't care where and exactly when our people do their job, as long as it gets done on time."

Maple Appleyard made a small gesture with her hand. "As far as Glen Gordon is concerned, he's been with FIS for five years, ever since he got out of college, and he's good at his work, so if he wants to work a few nights so he can get some days off, it's okay with us. He's got an excellent record, and he's very dependable."

Helen nodded. "I'm glad to hear that flextime works well for you. You say Glen Gordon has been with you for five years?"

Maple Appleyard nodded. "Ever since he got out of NYU. He was with our New York office for four years, then transferred up here." She allowed herself a smile. "I suspect it had something to do with a woman. Someone who lives in this area."

"But it was your gain, whatever his motive."

"Yes, indeed."

"I'm not a banker," I said. "Maybe you can tell me how you work with, say, Helen's bank. It might help me think a little straighter."

Maple Appleyard looked first at me, then at Helen.

"We're working together," said Helen.

"On something that involves FIS, I take it." Maple Appleyard was suddenly all business. "That makes it my business, too. Before I go much further, perhaps you'll enlighten me. What is this matter you're both involved in?"

Bankers and accountants, however reluctant they themselves are to impart information, are as eager as anyone else to get it. Maple Appleyard listened while Helen and I told her about the oddly large bank accounts of Kathy Ellis and Denise Vale, of the checks made out to the New Bedford, Woods Hole and Nantucket Salvage Company, and of the fact that both Kathy and Denise apparently knew Glen Gordon.

When we were done, she nodded. "I see. You want to talk to Glen Gordon to see what, if anything, he can tell you about those accounts. I'm sorry that he isn't here, but I'll make sure he contacts you when he comes in on Monday. Meanwhile, I will definitely take a look at them myself."

"How does the system work?" I asked. "Like I said, I know nothing about banking."

Again, Maple looked first at Helen. Then she leaned back in her chair and put her fingers together.

"We've done business with the Vineyard Haven National Bank for many years. However, the bank is now going to have its own computerized accounts and will no longer require our services. At the moment, we're transferring the accounts we've handled to the bank's new computer system.

"The system is called DDA, short for Demand Deposit Accounting. Every customer has an account with a particular number. A balance for that account remains constant until a withdrawal or a deposit is made, at which time the amount in the account is adjusted accordingly. Nothing else can change the balance in an account."

"Even you can understand that part, J. W.," said Helen, patting my knee.

Maple Appleyard allowed herself a small smile and went on. "The accounts are split up into cycles, and there are about a thousand accounts to a cycle. Everything has to balance. If anyone tries to alter the balance of the cycle by any means other than a legal deposit or withdrawal, the cycle will be out of balance and that fact will be noted instantly."

I raised my hand like a child who wants to go to the bathroom. "I read somewhere about somebody making a lot of money by stealing the cents from rounding down instead of rounding up. Lots of pennies nobody missed became lots of dollars that the guy really enjoyed spending until he got caught."

"I know that story," said Maple Appleyard. "But there isn't any rounding in DDA accounts. In all these years, we've never had any trouble at all with the Vineyard Haven National Bank accounts. They've always balanced to the penny."

"I agree," said Helen. "If somebody is stealing money from the bank, they're being pretty clever about it."

"Maybe so," I said, "but two college girls who can save a hundred thousand dollars apiece while they do summer work on Martha's Vineyard *are* pretty clever, wouldn't you say?"

"Maybe not as clever as you think," murmured Helen. "One of them is dead, remember, and the other is missing."

True. I looked at Maple Appleyard. "That's another reason I'd like to talk to Glen Gordon," I said. "He knew both of the girls personally. I think he may have been dating both of them."

She sat back. "And one of the girls is dead and the other one missing, you say. Tell me about that."

I did. She listened and then leaned forward and pressed a button on a speaker. "Bring in Glen Gordon's file, please."

A moment later, the secretary came in, placed a file on her desk, and went back out through the door. Maple Appleyard opened the file and flipped through it, then returned to the first page, which contained a photo. She turned the file toward us and we looked at the smiling face of a young man.

"That's our Glen Gordon. I can't imagine him being involved in the death or disappearance of anyone. Is that the man you're interested in?"

I decided not to point out that a lot of serial killers are guys most people couldn't imagine being involved in the deaths or disappearances of others. "I'm interested in Glen Gordon," I said, "but I don't know if that's him. I've never seen him or his picture. All I have is his name. Can I have a copy of this to show to some people on the Vineyard?"

Again, Maple Appleyard pressed the speaker button and gave quick directions to the secretary, who came in, took the photo, and went out again.

"There's a photo place just down the road," said Maple. "They owe me a favor."

"Can we look at the file?" I asked, pointing at the folder.

"Our files are confidential," she said, frowning.

"Then maybe you can give me some information that's in there. When did Glen graduate, and what was his major?"

She looked at the file and gave us the information. There wasn't much that was new. Glen Gordon was a math and computer major, and had indeed graduated five years earlier. We did get the home address and telephone number he'd given when applying for work at

FIS. If he was like most young college grads, he'd used his family's phone and address when making his application.

After a bit, the secretary came back with an envelope containing two copies of Glen Gordon's photograph. Maple Appleyard gave them to us, and Helen and I exchanged glances and stood up.

Maple Appleyard came around the desk to shake hands with us. "I'm going to be looking into this matter very seriously. I don't know that anything is wrong, but if there's anything illegal going on, I'll find out about it. If I can locate Glen, I'll talk to him immediately. I'll see him next Monday at the latest. Do keep me informed, and I'll contact you with any information relevant to this business."

Helen and I went out and got into Matt Jung's car. Helen looked at her watch. "Let's drive down to Falmouth and have a look at the P.O. box that belongs to the New Bedford et al. Salvage Company. We can turn up the collars of our trench coats and lean against the wall until somebody shows up to collect the mail, then we can either nail him on the spot or trail him back to his hideout."

"You're scary," I said.

We drove down to Falmouth and found the box, but we didn't see anyone come for the mail.

"I wish I had a badge," said Helen. "I'd go ask some questions about the people who use this box."

"It happens," I said, "that I do have a badge. Stand there and try to look like a policewoman."

Helen beamed and I went over to the window where the mail was handed out. The fact that my badge was the old one I'd used while I was on the Boston P.D. didn't make much difference. A badge is a badge to most people. I let the guy behind the window get a quick look at it, asked him if I could talk to him confidentially, then, in a very small voice, asked him about the people who used the box.

As people do when spoken to in small voices, he lowered his own. The box, he explained, was in the name of the New Bedford, Woods Hole and Nantucket Salvage Company. The people who used it were a man he thought he remembered being identified as the treasurer of the company and the woman who was his assistant. Nobody else used the box, as far as he knew. No, he didn't recognize the name Cecil Jones; no, there wasn't a lot of mail delivered in the box; and no, there wasn't any particular time of day when the mail was picked up.

I thanked him in my small voice and went back to Helen.

"Well?" she asked, as we went out.

"Zero," I said.

Back in Hyannis, we left Matt Jung's car behind his bank, and tried and failed to find Matt himself. Matt's videotape of Cecil Jones would have to be sent to us later. We ate sandwiches in the same café where we'd lunched, and walked to the dock where we caught the Hy-line back to the island. It was a lovely crossing, and I admired the soft summer sea while I wondered what I had learned during the day.

After delivering Helen back to her house in Vineyard Haven, I stopped by Beth Goodwin's place. Beth was still at work, so I didn't get my hands on her film either. More zero. I drove on home.

▪ 22 ▪

When I got out of the old Land Cruiser, I could hear the music coming from the house. Keyboard music. I thought I recognized something by Chopin. I wasn't anxious for it to stop, so I sat on the porch and listened.

It was clear that Dave was ready to go back to the world of music that he'd left so precipitously not many days before. The Vineyard can do that to you: revive you and make you well when another world has made you ill.

After a while the music ended, and I went inside.

Quinn was having a cognac and Dave was sipping a beer. There was a plate on the coffee table containing the remains of a fillet of smoked bluefish, some Brie, and some crackers.

"Sounded good," I said.

Dave flexed his fingers. "Got to get limbered up if I'm going to get out of the bullpen and back up on the mound."

"Are you ready to get up there again?"

"I am."

"Yes, he is," said Quinn. "Me, too, I guess. The first story I'm going to write, and the one that will endear me to my boss again after this disappearing act I just pulled, is going to be the true tale of David Greenstein's escape from the concert stage. It'll be a genuine scoop, and I'll be back in everybody's good graces."

"Except my manager's, of course," smiled Dave.

"Hey, my golden prose will even win his hard heart," said Quinn. "You're going to emerge as a really terrific guy. Your manager will love me. Your fans will love you. The concert organizers will sell more tickets than ever before. The record companies will pay you a fortune for new disks. Women will swoon when they hear your name. You'll be right up there with Elvis. It's going to be terrific, and all because of me."

"Immortality," I said to Dave. "And you're still so young."

"Another god in the celestial hierarchy," agreed Dave. "When it's destiny, you can't fight it."

"When are you headed back? When does the triumphal march begin?"

"I have a car reservation on the 7 A.M. boat the day after tomorrow," said Quinn.

"It's really been good down here," said Dave. "I'll be back."

I too had come down to the island to get away from a world taut with pressure. But though the island had cured us both, I, unlike Dave, had no plans to return whence I'd come.

"And what have you been up to?" asked Quinn.

I told them about my day.

"Ah," said Quinn. "Possible skulduggery afoot. Do you need an ace reporter's inquiring mind and dogged patience to help you figure out what's going on?"

"I thought you were on vacation."

"That was earlier," said Quinn. "Like Dave, here, I'm going back to work and I need to warm up first."

"In spite of your efforts to be lazy, you're a born drone."

"The fourth estate is my kingdom, and I live to serve. What do you need to know that you don't know?"

"You're serious."

"Yeah. I'm going to be here one more day, you've got a phone, and I've got a card that lets me charge calls to the office. While Dave, here, flexes his fingers and gets his piano muscles back in shape, I can make some calls and maybe get some information you need but don't have. Who knows? I might be able to get a story out of it."

Quinn was a very good reporter. He was gifted with a nose that could sniff the faintest smells of vice, and claws that could dig up secrets buried deep.

I thought about all the things I didn't know.

"Okay," I said. "Tomorrow you can make some calls."

Quinn looked happy. "Good. Now sit down and join me in a snort of this brandy while you sample that blue and Brie. Perfectly smoked bluefish, if I say so myself." He waved an airy hand at Dave. "Maestro, a little drinking and digesting music, if you please."

Dave grinned, sipped his beer, then set the glass aside and touched the keys. Music filled the room. I sat down. Cognac, hors d'oeuvres, and David Greenstein at the keyboard. Not bad.

The next morning, early, I wrote down what I knew about the case, then went to Beth Goodwin's house before she could escape again. She wiped the sleep from her eyes and gave me a photograph of a girl and a young man. I recognized the girl as being Kathy Ellis. I recognized the young man, too. Glen Gordon. He looked just like the guy in the picture I'd gotten yesterday from Maple Appleyard.

"I hope that helps," said Beth Goodwin, yawning and holding her robe together at her throat.

"It does," I said. "Now I know that this Glen Gordon is the same Glen Gordon as the one who works over at Frazier Information Systems. It's not much, but it's something I couldn't be sure of before."

At home, I found Quinn and Dave having coffee and eating smoked bluefish, red onion, and cream cheese on bagels. A world-class breakfast. I joined them. Delish.

"All right," said Quinn, when he finally pushed himself back from the table. "I'm ready to roll. What do you want to know?"

"I want you to dig up whatever you can about Glen Gordon, Cecil Jones, and the New Bedford, Woods Hole and Nantucket Salvage Company. While you're at it, you might try to find out where Denise Vale is, and the tie-in between her and Kathy Ellis and Glen Gordon and Cecil Jones."

"You don't want much," said Quinn. "Have you ever considered becoming a city editor? You have the gall for it. I take it that you want to see how all this stuff hooks together."

"Correct." I gave him the notes I'd written. "Here's what I have to get you started. Events, names, addresses, and telephone numbers. Helen Fine will help you out with the money part, and I think Matt Jung and Maple Appleyard will, too, although they may be shy about talking to a reporter."

"I know the type. What I'll do is get as much background stuff as I can, then I'll start looking to see where the money comes from and goes. The old silver trail is always a good one to follow."

"Even though I'm already a dedicated professional in another field, I'd be glad to help you out," said Dave. "Unfortunately, J. W. only has one phone, so I guess I'll just have to get back to the old keyboard, then go out into the yard for a final sun-bronzing before tomorrow's return to reality."

"In your spare time," I said, "you can come up with some winning information about staying in good with a Portuguese mother-in-law. I know I'd do fine if you were always on hand to soothe her with song, but tomorrow you'll be gone and I'll be here all alone. Give it some thought. I clearly need help."

"Maybe not so much as you think," said Dave, getting up and carrying dishes to the kitchen.

I looked after him. Maybe he was right. One thing for sure: although marrying Zee didn't mean I had to marry her family, too, things would be a lot better if I was also on good terms with her kin, if that was possible. I hadn't met Dad or the brothers yet, so I couldn't do much about them; but Maria was right here. Round one with her hadn't been a good one for me, but round two had been a lot better—thanks, admittedly, to Quinn's and Dave's collective charms. Round three was coming up soon, somewhere, sometime. Better to take the bull by the horns, I decided. I put a rod on the roof rack, got into the Land Cruiser, and drove up to Zee's house.

Zee answered her door. She looked terrific in shorts and tee shirt, her long blue-black hair knotted in a kerchief on her head. She held some gauzy-looking blue material in her hand. Behind her, I could see Maria, glasses on her nose, looking at me over some sewing.

"You're ravishing," I said, loudly.

"Thank you," said Zee.

"Oh," I said, looking down at her. "You too. Like mother, like daughter."

Zee patted my cheek pretty hard and kissed me. "I don't think you should really woo Mom. What if you won her?"

"It's all right, dear," said Maria, getting up and coming to meet me. "Let him talk. I love it." She gave me a kiss that was not entirely maternal.

"You can take turns caring for me as I grow old," I said. "It'll be great." I went in and looked around the room. It was tumbled with what seemed to be yards of lace and cloth the color of the sky just where it touches the sea—a sort of pale violet. "I take it that the wedding is still on go. Is this all something I'm not supposed to see until the magic day?"

"No secrets here," said Zee. "If you could sew, we'd ask you to sit down and pitch in."

"Oh, dear," said Maria. "You mean you can't sew, Jefferson? Zeolinda will have to teach you after you're married." She looked at Zee. "Married men always have a lot to learn."

I also looked at Zee. "What do you mean, 'If you could sew'? I can sew." I glanced at Maria. "I even have a sewing machine. I salvaged it at the Edgartown dump years ago. Almost as good as new. All it needed was a little TLC and new switch. Runs like a charm."

"All true," said Zee to her mother. "The only thing missing from that picture is sewing skill."

"I can sew things together," I said.

"If you don't mind how they look," said Zee. "But if you do mind, it's another story. Except for sails. For some reason, Mom, he can sew a good seam on a sail, I'll give him that." She gestured at the piles of cloth. "I don't think this is your sort of game, Jeff."

"Oh, you mean it's woman's work, I suppose? A sexist attitude if ever I heard one."

Zee tossed her head and smiled. Certain of my glands began to dance.

"Why don't you ladies abandon this project, and let me take you for a ride out to Cape Pogue? Do you good to get some fresh air." I looked at Maria. "Have you ever been on the four-wheel-drive tour on the Chappy beaches? No? Tsk, tsk. Your daughter hasn't been entertaining you properly. Put away that needle and grab your shades and your camera, and we'll be off."

Zee and her mother exchanged looks, and Zee put her sewing down. "I'll get my rod and tackle box!"

Most of the hundred thousand or so summer people who come to the Vineyard each year never see the faraway parts of the island that can be reached only with a four-wheel-drive vehicle. Principal among these wild and lovely distant places are the beaches of Chappaquiddick, where the fishermen roam in pursuit of the fruits of the sea.

We drove down to Katama, took a left onto the sands flattened by Hurricane Bob, and drove along the barrier beach between the blue Atlantic and Katama Bay. The beach was just beginning to fill with that day's June People anxious to improve their tans, but out in the bay the pro quahoggers and clammers were already at work on the flats.

The first land to the south of the beach was probably the Dominican Republic, but north of the clammers, through the narrows, we could see Edgartown. Along the beach were birds: terns, gulls, and two pairs of oyster catchers who had a nest in what remained of the beach grass.

We reached Chappaquiddick, that sometimes island that was then, as it usually is, hooked to the rest of the Vineyard by the barrier beach, and drove along the road through the dunes, climbing the wooden road, crossing the boardwalk, and passing Swan Lake. No otters in the lake today, but plenty of ducks and cormorants, and two pairs of swans. We came out onto the beach where the Jeeps were lined up between Leland's and Wasque points. The rods were mostly vertical and the fishermen were standing around drinking coffee and talking, so it was clear that the bluefish were not there in the famous Wasque Rip.

"Alas," said Zee. "But good luck for you, Mom, because if the fish were in, this might be the end of your tour."

I cut inside to Pocha Pond and took the sandy road through some of the world-champion poison ivy that grows on the dunes, toward the Dike Bridge where, more than a score of years before, America's most famous automobile accident had taken place. As we approached it, Zee pointed it out to Maria.

"You know about the supposed pieces of the true cross that were so popular with Christians in medieval times? Some wag said that if they actually were all pieces of the cross, it would have had to have been two miles high. Anyway, we call this the True Bridge, because there actually are people who have come and cut pieces off it as relics."

"You don't say."

"We can get you one, if you want."

"No thank you, dear. I'm a Republican, but I'm not a sick Republican."

"It gets worse. Did you know that some people have come here and dipped up water from beneath the bridge and taken it home in vials, like holy water?"

"Don't be blasphemous, sweetheart."

"I'm not the blasphemer, I'm just the reporter. There also used to be a guy who came down here on the anniversary of the accident and held prayer services in memory of it all. What do you think of that?"

"I hope he wasn't Catholic."

I had to laugh. "I don't think he was. I think he was one of those fundamentalist Bible thumpers. Anyway, as you can see, there's almost nothing left of the bridge, now. You can't even walk across it. They say they're going to build a new one. If they do, maybe the curiosity seekers will stop coming. That would make a lot of Chappy people happy, for sure. Their roads have been filled with bridge hunters for twenty years, and they're tired of them."

We drove to Cape Pogue Pond, where the Vineyard's largest quahogs live, and where we do some of the best scalloping in New England. There were snowy egrets along the beach, and a great blue heron was wading in the shallow water. We drove on to the lighthouse, then down along the beach, past the gull nesting area, to the Cape Pogue Gut.

To the north, across the blue water, were the Oak Bluffs bluffs. Beyond them and to the east, on the far side of the sound, and under a file of gray-white clouds, was the hazy line of land that was Cape Cod. To the west we could see the white houses of Edgartown. Sailboats, going before a gentle southwest wind, were heading out. Over everything, the blue summer sky arched from horizon to horizon.

There were more fishermen at the gut, but again there were no fish.

"Wrong time and tide," explained Zee.

"If you knew that," said Maria, "why did you bring your fishing poles?"

"Because," said Zee, "you never really, absolutely know for sure. And can you imagine what it would be like to get down here without a rod and find out that the fish are blitzing? No, no, Mom. One never goes onto the beach without one's rod. Jeff taught me that."

"It was a business deal," I said. "I'd teach her how to fish, and she'd marry me."

"I see," said Maria.

When we got back to Cape Pogue, we took the outer beach to the Jetties, then hooked back inside. To complete the tour, we cut up onto Chappy and caught the On Time ferry back across to Edgartown.

"Very lovely," said Maria when we were back at Zee's house. "I had no idea there were such beautiful, wild places on the island. But wouldn't you know it? I didn't take a single picture!"

"We'll make a special photography tour," I said. "Whenever you want."

Zee walked me to the Land Cruiser.

"You are a smoothie," she said, squeezing my arm.

"Endless flattery," I said. "That's the secret of winning women. That's how I got you, after all."

"Consider yourself whacked with a stick," said Zee, kissing me good-bye.

I drove to Vineyard Haven and went to see Helen Fine. She beckoned me into her office.

"I've been trying to call you, but your line's been busy all morning. We have an interesting development on our hands. Matt Jung sent a tape across on an early boat, and I had Eddie set up the TV. I want you to see this."

A television set and a VCR were sitting on a table across from Helen's desk. She picked up a remote control, and the TV screen lit up. A moment later, fuzzy shapes appeared. A time and a date were in the upper corner of the picture. The fuzzy shapes became people doing business at teller windows in a bank. After a bit, the movement stopped and a particular man at a window was highlighted. A voice on the tape identified the man as Cecil Jones. A moment later, there was a blowup of the man's face.

I must have made some sort of sound.

"Indeed," said Helen Fine. "Here." She handed me her copy of the photograph Maple Appleyard had given us the day before. I looked at it and then at the TV screen and then at Helen.

"No doubt about it," I said.

She nodded. "Glen Gordon and Cecil Jones are the same person." She put her palms together and smiled a humorless smile. "I think the pot has just begun to boil."

■ 23 ■

Why was I not surprised? Because Miles the medic was also Miles the bully? Because all of us wear more than one face? Because this stew seemed to be in a small pot where there wasn't much room for any ingredients but the essentials?

I wondered what Quinn was finding out. The actors in the drama I was investigating were beginning to look like bugs in a web. One of them was the spider, but which one?

On the television screen, the enlarged picture of Cecil Jones/Glen Gordon went away and there was more fuzzy film of other customers at teller windows. Then the tape highlighted a male customer who used a cane and seemed to favor a stiff left leg. The film stopped, and there was another highlighted photo of that male customer, followed by a blowup of the face. The voice identified this man, too, as Cecil Jones. And having had the face identified, I could see that it was, indeed, the same man. But this face wore sideburns and a small moustache. The voice explained that this Cecil Jones always did business at the Sandwich branch office, where he was known. The film went on, and a third Cecil Jones was shown doing business at the Chatham branch office. This Cecil wore wire-rimmed glasses, had a neat beard, and parted his hair on the other side of his head. The Provincetown Cecil was the same as the Hyannis Cecil.

Helen stopped the tape. "That's all there is about Cecil Jones. Three Cecils for four banks. Why did he bother?"

Why, indeed? I guessed. "Because if ID time ever arrives, in court, for example, it'll be just that much harder to get witnesses to agree about who it was that took out the money. A good lawyer could make a lot out of that."

"Even though the prosecution would have this film?"

"There was no way Cecil could keep from being filmed. All he could do was make things confusing. And even if he doesn't fool anybody, there's no law against changing the way you look when you make bank withdrawals, is there?"

"None that I know of."

"Have you seen the rest of the film?"

"Yes. There are pictures of Marilyn Grimes, the assistant treasurer, making withdrawals. The same person every time. Makes me wonder if maybe she was also being suckered by Cecil."

"Let's have a look at her."

The film ran and a highlighted Marilyn Grimes appeared. She wore thick glasses and graying hair in a severe hairdo. Her blouse was buttoned to the neck, and her jacket and skirt were, even to my ignorant eyes, far out of fashion. She had prominent upper teeth that made her look weak in the chin. She never smiled, but attended to her work and departed.

"How old?" I asked Helen.

She shrugged. "Thirties? Forties? It's hard to tell. Matt probably has her age in his records. You recognize her?"

"No. Her face is a type you see, though."

"What do you mean?"

"I started noticing facial types when I was a kid. Later on, it paid off sometimes when I was a cop. Anyway, start looking at faces, and you'll see what I mean. There are some archetypal faces that appear over and over again. Certain movie actors and actresses have those faces, and you can see the same faces in ordinary people. There's the Brando face, for example. The young Brando. The eyes, the shape of the skull and face, even the hairline. There's the James Dean face. That forehead, those eyes and lips, that jawline. I've seen a lot of those faces in jail, incidentally. There's the Katharine Hepburn face. You see it around the island in the summertime, but not often. There's the Paul Newman face, and the Bette Davis face.

"This woman, Marilyn Grimes, has a face I recognize, but don't remember. The Wicked Witch of the West, maybe?"

"Look some more. Maybe it'll come to you."

There were three other films and close-ups of Marilyn Grimes, all taken at the Hyannis office. Marilyn apparently did not do business at the other branches. She also apparently didn't own any other clothes.

After I'd seen all of the pictures, I still didn't know who she was.

"I've started some wheels turning," said Helen. "I'm trying to find out if any other of our customers have written checks that were deposited by the New Bedford, Woods Hole and Nantucket Salvage Company. I think I'm about to contact some people who investigate possible fraud."

"Good idea. Bring in the pros."

She had a concerned look on her face. "Your nose isn't going to be out of joint, is it? I mean, you're the one who got us going on this thing. Now, some other guys may go with it and maybe get the credit."

I almost laughed, but she looked so serious that I managed not to. "No," I said. "My nose isn't going to be out of joint. I'm not in the cop business any longer. What's more, in a couple of weeks, I'm going to be a married man, and I plan on concentrating on that, not on Glen Gordon and his friends. Your investigators can have the job."

And I meant it, too. At least until I got home and heard what Quinn had to say.

Dave was sleeping in the yard on the plastic lounger that I'd gotten for almost nothing in a yard sale. It's amazing what some people will throw away or sell for peanuts. I have a lot of it around my place.

Quinn was on the phone and had a pile of notes in front of him. He looked cheerful. In spite of his claims that he was born to be retired, Quinn was happiest when he was plying his trade. He waved at me, talked some more, and put down the phone.

"Guess what?"

"What?"

"The New Bedford, Woods Hole and Nantucket Salvage Company doesn't seem to have any assets but a telephone in a rented room and a mailbox. You don't seem shocked. On the other hand, it's a legit outfit as far as the law is concerned. It's got two members: Cecil Jones and Marilyn Grimes. Nobody else. The phone is hooked to an answering machine that I got every time I tried it. The room is over in Falmouth. Here's the address. How did I get that information? I have friends in various organizations who owe me little favors. Friends who owe favors or want them are a reporter's best buddies."

"I have some news for you, too," I said, and I told him about Glen Gordon being Cecil Jones.

"Well, well," said Quinn.

"Have you found Denise Vale?" I asked.

"No. Is finding her high on your list of priorities?"

"All I know is that Kathy Ellis was a friend of Glen Gordon, or Cecil Jones, or whoever he's calling himself these days, that she had a Vineyard Haven National Bank checking account with a lot of money in it, that she took the money out and Cecil Jones deposited it in his salvage company account over on the Cape, and that now Kathy is dead. The same is true of Denise Vale, except so far Denise is only missing. What does that make you think?"

"That Denise Vale is missing because she's also dead?"

"It seems to be a possibility."

"At the hands of . . . ?"

"Cecil Jones seems to have ended up with the money."

"Cherchez la gelt." Quinn nodded. "Glen, as Cecil, gets the gold, and the girls get the ax. Or in this case, the poison."

"Sex, greed, or fear were motives for most of the murders I know about."

Quinn looked through his notes. "Here we are. Denise Vale didn't show up for work at the Fireside over the weekend. That means she's been missing for at least a week. Plenty of time to get herself killed."

I nodded. "Or to go to Rio de Janeiro, or to start writing the great American novel, or to do a lot of other things, or have a lot of other things happen to her."

Quinn nodded. "Keerect, partner. One never knows, does one?" His fingers worked their way through some more notes. "I do have some stuff about her. Called her folks. First Mom, then Dad. Told them I was doing a feature on the careers of some typical NYU grads. Got the usual stuff—year of graduation; major—Denise was in business administration, by the way. A very sharp student; interests—Denise was interested in the theater for a while and in making money all of the time. But she's had a hard time finding work in these tough times, so she's been doing a little of this and a little of that. Jealous dad, protective mom—you know about that. I got the impression that she plays one off against the other when it serves her purposes to do it. Right now, she seems to be sided with Mom.

"Did you know she lived for a while with our friend Glen Gordon? Her senior year, apparently. Lived in the dorm her first two years, then had her own apartment, then lived with him in his."

"Did you talk to anybody at the dorm?"

"No. Why?"

"Her mom mentioned some problem there, but never said what it was."

"According to what I hear," said Quinn, "college students have three main kinds of problems: roommate problems, parent problems, and problems with boyfriends and girlfriends. Academic problems are last on the list. Usually, if somebody flunks out, it's because of one of the first three problems. But I'll check it out.

"Nothing to explain how she managed to get all that money into her checking account, by the way. That's about all I got on Denise."

He went through more notes. "Ah, here's Kathy Ellis. Nice girl. Middle-class people. Both schoolteachers. She was the romantic, idealistic type, according to her parents. Vegetarian, peace movements, Victorian poetry, theater, that sort of thing. Very nice, but the kind who loves not wisely but too well. Broke up with her high school beau when she went to college. Shattered her Freshman Heart. Met you know who—Glen Gordon— at a college theater production. He was doing the lights or something technical, and she was an actress. She was swept away. Brought him home over a holiday. Her parents liked him.

"No explanation for the money in her account. Her parents were shocked when I suggested that she had a good deal of dough, since she was working and saving every penny for college. An unsolved mystery.

"Now, here's our friend Glen 'Gordy' Gordon. A real charmer, according to everybody I talked to. Smart, too. Majored in math and computers. Went to work for Frazier Information Systems in New Jersey. Last year, he transferred up here to Hyannis. Kathy Ellis was pretty happy when he did, since she was working here on the island for the summer. They dated steadily. When she died, I hear that he was really broken up."

I had heard the same thing from Beth Goodwin. "What did you learn about FIS?"

Quinn lifted a thumb. "Straight-arrow outfit. Fine reputation. They do accounting work for various firms, and have connections with a lot of banks in the North Atlantic region. Glen Gordon is a rising star, apparently. Has a real touch for the trade." His mouth kinked at one corner. "Of course they probably never heard of Cecil Jones or the New Bedford etcetera Salvage Company, so their perception of old Gordy might not be as sharp as maybe yours or maybe mine."

"Why did he transfer up to Hyannis?"

"Something about liking the area, and there being a guy up here who wanted to go down there. They sort of traded places. FIS is pretty big on being flexible, as you know."

"Do you know where he's living on the Cape?"

"As a matter of fact, I do. It helps to have tipsters working for the phone company. If I can get his number, I can get his address. He's got an apartment in Woods Hole, about two jumps from the steamship authority docks."

Some recollection was working in the back of my head. I couldn't quite grasp it, but it seemed to me that it would help me if I could get a hand on it. I set the hounds of my brain to track down the elusive memory, and returned to Quinn.

"Is Gordy at home?" I asked.

"Just his answering machine. Incidentally, I notice that you don't have one of your own. What are you, a communications Neanderthal or something? Everybody has an answering machine these days."

Just then, the phone rang.

"It's for me," said Quinn. "I left your number with some people." He put the phone to his ear. "Quinn here." He listened, then said, "Just a minute," and handed the phone to me.

Bonzo was calling from the Fireside. "Hey, J. W., how you doing?"

"I'm doing okay, Bonzo. What's up?"

"Well, I'm at work here, you know, sweeping up and like that, and you know what?"

"No. What?"

"You remember that girl you came in here looking for?"

"Denise Vale?"

"Yeah, Denise. Well, you know you were looking for

her and she wasn't here, then you and that man got into that fight? Well, guess what?''

''What?''

''She's here again. She's back at work. Denise is working here right this very now.''

I thanked him, hung up, and looked at Quinn. ''The girl we buried has risen from her grave. Denise Vale is back on the island.''

▪ 24 ▪

Dave Greenstein was getting pretty toasted when I left the house. I suggested to Quinn that he either put an umbrella over him or wake him up and have him come inside. Otherwise, Dave would be so sunburned when he got back to Boston that he'd have to take another vacation to recover.

In Oak Bluffs, I found a parking place at the far end of Circuit Avenue and walked back to the Fireside. It was lunchtime, but most people don't go to the Fireside to eat unless they plan to pig out on bar food and beer. Not a bad meal, come to think of it.

There were half a dozen men sitting at tables drinking, and I saw Bonzo in the back room, taking rubbish out to the barrels behind the building. There was a woman behind the bar polishing glasses and setting them where she could get at them again when she needed them. The Fireside wasn't the kind of place where a lot of people drank their beer out of glasses, but there were always exceptions to the rule. The woman no longer had the freshman glow that she'd had in her father's photograph, but when I looked at her carefully I could see that she was Denise Vale.

I sat down at the bar and ordered a bottle of Sam Adams and, just to show I wasn't an ordinary guy, a glass to go with it. When she came back with the beer,

I said, "Glad to see you back. Your dad was getting worried."

She looked at me. Her voice, when she spoke, had no more expression than her face. "Who are you?"

"J. W. Jackson. I've been looking for you."

"Well, now you can stop looking." She moved back to her towel and glasses.

I got up and moved to a stool closer to her. "You've been gone for a week, Denise. Lots of people have been worried about you. Your dad, your roommates. Where have you been?"

She didn't look up or pause in her polishing. "I'm a big girl. People don't have to worry about me. I had some business to take care of, and now I'm back. That's the whole story. You go back and tell that to my loving daddy."

"What kind of business?"

"None that's any of yours. Go drink your beer and let me do my work."

I drank some of my Sam Adams. Still America's finest bottled beer.

"I'd really like to know where you've been, Denise. And there's another thing. I'm trying to get a line on a friend of yours, a guy named Glen Gordon, also known as Gordy. I thought maybe you could give me some information about him."

"You thought wrong."

"You can talk to me or you can talk to other people. The cops, maybe."

That feeble ploy got me a glance, at least. "What are you talking about? Why would the cops want to talk with me?"

A good question, actually. "Glen Gordon had a girlfriend named Kathy Ellis. Last week Kathy ended up dead. Poisoned. When a woman is killed, the first people the cops like to talk to are husbands and boyfriends. Glen Gordon and you were close, and maybe you still are. Ergo, when the cops decide to talk to Glen, they'll want to talk to you, too."

Denise kept on polishing glasses, but now she was looking at me. "What makes you think Kathy Ellis was killed? I heard that it was an accident. That she was always eating wild plants and that this time she ate the wrong thing."

"Maybe, maybe not. You knew Kathy, too, so that's another reason the cops will want to talk to you."

Two customers came in and sat at the end of the bar. She went and got their orders. Two beers, of course. No glasses. When she'd served them, she came back to me.

"If the cops wanted to talk to me, they'd have done it by now."

"I don't think they know what I know about the tie-ins between you and Glen and Kathy, but they will as soon as I tell them. Of course, I may not have to tell them."

"You mean you're the only one who knows?"

"So far," I lied.

She thought for a while, then she said, "Look, Glen Gordon and I haven't been together for a long time, so I can't tell you anything about him. I heard he had another girl, but I didn't know he was seeing Kathy Ellis. The other thing you want to know is where I've been. Well, I've been over in New Bedford. There's another man in my life now, and I've been over there with him. We had a row awhile back and we needed some time to patch it up." She stopped polishing and looked at me hard. "That's what you wanted to know, isn't it? Now you don't have to go to the cops. I don't need to have the cops in my life right now."

"There are a few other things we need to talk about, Denise."

"What, for God's sake? Look, I've got work to do." She gestured. Sure enough, more customers were coming in.

"Do you know a man named Cecil Jones?"

"Excuse me." She went along the bar and served more beer to the newcomers, then came back. "Who'd you say?"

"Cecil Jones."

"Who's Cecil Jones?"

"You never heard the name?"

"No."

"Did you ever hear of the New Bedford, Woods Hole and Nantucket Salvage Company?"

She studied me carefully, then shook her head. "No. Should I have?"

"Probably."

"Well, I never heard of them." She moved away and served more beer to some men at a table. Beer was clearly the drink of choice among the noontime regulars. I was pleased to know that my Sam Adams put me in the social mainstream.

Denise came back. "Things are getting busy. You know everything you need to know?"

"There's only one other thing. The money."

Her eyes changed. "What do you mean?"

"I mean, where did you get a hundred thousand dollars? Why did you write a check for that amount to cash? And who did you give the check to?"

For the first time, Denise looked worried. "What do you mean?"

"I mean I know about the money that was in your account. I mean I want to know where it came from and where it went and how you figure in the scam."

Denise put her hands on the bar as if to steady herself. She dropped her head and put her lower lip between her teeth and stared at the floor. She took some deep breaths.

From down the bar came a call for service. Denise didn't move. The call came again, still good-natured, but louder. Denise looked toward the would-be beer drinker, then at me. "I can't talk about that now," she said in a tight voice. "I'll tell you everything, but it's going to take some time. You'll have to see me when I get off work."

"When do you get off?"

"Midnight."

"I'll be here."

"Hey, lady," called the guy down the bar, "you love-birds can bill and coo on your own time. How about a beer?"

Denise went to get his order and I finished my Sam Adams and went out. At the door, I paused and looked back. Denise Vale was watching me. There was no expression on her face.

I walked up to the corner, took a left, then another left, and walked until I was behind the Fireside. Bonzo was pushing trash barrels around. He beamed when he saw me.

"Hey, J. W., I seen you and Denise talking. She's back, just like I told you. Say, J. W., when can we go fishing again? I'd sure like to catch another fish. My mom likes to eat the ones I catch, you know."

Bonzo's mother was a teacher at the high school. During the summer she waited tables. Sweet, mindless Bonzo was her heart's delight.

"We'll go fishing soon," I said. "Say, Bonzo, how late are you working today?"

Bonzo frowned. "Oh, I can't go fishing today, J. W. I got to work until we close. Hey, I even got to work after that. Cleaning up, you know. I like to do some of the cleaning up at night so I don't have to do so much the next morning. I mean, look at all this work I'm doing right now. This is stuff that I didn't get done last night, and you can see there's a lot of it still to do."

"I can see that. I want you to do something for me, Bonzo. I'm supposed to meet Denise here at midnight so we can have a talk. If she has to leave before that, I want you to call me right away. Okay?"

He nodded and gave me his childish smile. "Yeah, J. W., I can do that. It would be a pleasure."

I thanked him and went home. Dave was now inside, out of the sun. He was reading the *Globe* and having a beer. Quinn was still on the phone.

"It's safe for me to go back to Boston," said Dave, looking up. "Only one guy killed in town last night. Shot

in the Drago Hotel by a woman thought to be a prosti-
tute. Cops figure it for robbery. They're looking for her
now. Since I don't even know where the Drago Hotel is,
I guess I'll be okay."

"Unless you hire the same hooker," I said. Unlike
Dave, Quinn and I did know where the Drago was. Back
when I'd been on the Boston P.D., the Drago was already
pretty seedy. It wasn't the kind of hotel the chamber of
commerce talked about.

"There's a message for you," said Quinn, putting his
hand over the speaker, then pointing to a scrap of paper.

Helen Fine had called to say that Matt Jung had called
her to say that yesterday afternoon Marilyn Grimes had
made a cash withdrawal of all but a hundred dollars
from the New Bedford, Woods Hole and Nantucket Salvage Company account. If memory served me correctly,
that meant that Marilyn had walked out with a tad over
a hundred grand. All told, the company account had
been emptied of two hundred thousand dollars in the
past few weeks, all in cash.

When Quinn hung up, I told him about my day.

"Ah," said Quinn. "The old meet-me-at-midnight-
and-all-will-be-revealed ploy, eh? As I recall, the naive
investigator usually gets himself killed when he goes to
meet the informant, or else finds the informant dead and
himself the suspect for murder. I've seen it a dozen times
on the late show."

"Hey," said Dave, who had gotten to the Arts and
Entertainment section of the paper. "Look here. A little
story saying I'll be back in town tomorrow, and that the
mystery of where I've been is expected to be revealed.
Now how did the paper get that information, Quinn?"

Quinn took the newspaper and looked at the story.
"Pretty much the way I phoned it in. And more to come
tomorrow, when I will reveal all. A Quinn exclusive."

My back hurt and I put a hand back there by my bullet. "I don't want any goddamned reporters coming
down my driveway, Quinn. You tell everybody where

Dave's been hiding out and there'll be pilgrims of all sorts crawling around this place."

"Don't worry," said Quinn. "When I say I'll reveal all, I don't really mean I'll reveal *all*. What I mean is I'll reveal almost all. Dave here will have spent his week staying with a reclusive Vineyard friend whose identity and location will be kept confidential. Okay?"

"Okay."

"Because," said Quinn, "Dave and I may want to come back again someday, and we'll need some peace and quiet."

"I'll be a married man by then, but I think Dave will be welcome anytime he wants to come. I don't know about you, Quinn. Zee may want me to start mixing with a better class of people."

"Nonsense. Zee loves me. The only reason she's marrying you is so she can be sure I'll keep coming around."

I had a thought, and took the paper from his hand. I read the Arts and Entertainment section through. There wasn't any rock and roll concert in Boston the coming weekend. Hmmmmm. I also read the story about the murder. There wasn't much. Name withheld until notification of kin. Room had been rented by the woman, who had been seen entering it with the man. She was missing. An investigation was under way. I was glad I had given up being a cop.

"You look pensive," said Quinn. "While you're in that mood, I'll give you the results of my latest investigative reporting.

"When Denise Vale first went to college, she lived in a dorm. But during her sophomore year, she and another girl got in a brawl over some mutual boyfriend, and Denise belted the girl with a flat iron and put her in the hospital. After that, Denise lived in an apartment. All that's from her mom, by the way. While I was chasing that story down, I went after some more names in this case. Guess who also attended NYU? Cecil Jones and Marilyn Grimes. Everybody involved in this caper went to the same college at about the same time. Interesting, no?"

Interesting, yes. "Were you able to find out where Cecil and Marilyn went after they graduated? Did they come to Cape Cod, for instance?"

"According to the notes you gave me, they're over there right now, running this phony-looking salvage company."

"Yeah, but we know that the guy who calls himself Glen Gordon is the same guy who calls himself Cecil Jones. He can't really be both of them."

Dave looked first at Quinn and then at me.

I rubbed my sore back. I didn't like it being sore. "If the real Marilyn knew the real Cecil and the real Glen Gordon at college, and if the real Marilyn is the person making deposits and withdrawals from the Zimmerman bank, and if she's not a crook herself, it means that the treasurer of the salvage company is the real Cecil and is just pretending to be Glen Gordon in his other life. But that's not likely, because the real Glen Gordon has been working for Frazier Information Systems for five years, and I'm sure that FIS must have checked up on Gordon's identity before they gave him the job. That means that the guy Marilyn knows as Cecil is really Glen, which means that either she didn't know Glen or Cecil in college, or she knows the man she's working with isn't the real Cecil, which means she's a crook, too."

Quinn nodded happily. "Yeah. And the two other names in this case, Denise Vale and Kathy Ellis, are NYU people, too, and we know they knew each other and that both of them knew Glen Gordon. All these people seemed to know each other. I think I'll give the Alumni Office a call, and see if I can get current addresses for Cecil and Glen and Marilyn. This witches' brew is getting complicated."

"Now, let me see if I've got this right," said Dave. "You've got one guy who calls himself by two names, and a woman who works with him when he uses one of those names, but who knows that it's a false one. They run a company that may be a fake, but have managed to get two hundred thousand dollars from the checking accounts of two island girls each of whom had no business having a hundred thousand dollars in her checking account, but who withdrew that money in checks made out to cash that were deposited in the Zimmerman bank by the guy with two names; then later the money was withdrawn in cash from the bank by the guy or the woman who knows one of his names is false."

"You have a good memory," I said. "Now I understand how you can play all those songs without ever looking at the music."

"And one of the island girls is now dead."

"Yes."

"And nobody really knows where Glen Gordon or Cecil Jones or whatever he calls himself is?"

"We know where he isn't," I said. "He's not in Boston attending a rock concert, like he said he was going to be."

"That means he might be over here on the island. I think I'd be careful, if I were you. And I think that Denise Vale should be careful, too."

I thought about that, and decided that Dave might be right. Before I left the house, I dug out my old police revolver and stuck it under my belt. To hide it, I wore my Black Dog sweatshirt. Deadly but stylish, that was me.

■ 25 ■

At a quarter to twelve I went into the Fireside. The place was loud, and the crowd was younger than the noon bunch. The smells of liquor and grass and sweaty bodies filled the air, and music blasted from the jukebox while voices tried to speak over it. I got a beer from Jackie, the bartender's wife, who clearly remembered the fight with Miles and wanted me to be happy. Down at the other end of the bar, Denise was earning her keep.

At midnight, Jackie rang a ship's bell, and service stopped. People who had finished their drinks and could get no more began to drift out. People who still had drinks stayed where they were. Denise took off her apron, got her purse, and ducked out under the bar. I finished my beer and met her at the door. We went out together.

She barely looked at me. "You have a car?"

"I have an aging Land Cruiser." I pointed up Circuit Avenue. From other bars, noisy patrons were coming out onto the street.

"We'll take that. There's a housing development off the County Road. It never got finished. Nobody will bother us there, and we can talk all night if we need to, and we might."

We walked up the street and got into the Land Cruiser and went out of the back of town. When we got to the

County Road, she pointed left and we headed toward
the airport. She said nothing more until we came to a
dirt road leading to the right. Then she said, "Turn
here."

I turned, and we drove over the bumpy road, passing
branch roads that were more overgrown than the one
we were on. It was dark as the pit.

We got to a circle at the end of the lane, and she said,
"This will be okay."

I drove around the circle until the Land Cruiser was
pointed out again, then stopped and killed the lights and
engine.

"Let's get out," she said. "I can use some air."

We got out. I got my flashlight and found us a log to
sit on. The moon was thin, and it was very dark. The
flashlight showed beer cans and other garbage around
us.

"Kids come here," she said. "Nobody bothers them.
Nobody can hear them. If they could hear them, they'd
bother them. That's the way people are. You have a cig-
arette?"

"No. I don't smoke."

I flicked off the flashlight, and the darkness fell in on
us. Gradually, my eyes adjusted. We were in a clearing
cut out of the woods. At one time, some developer had
spent a lot of money (someone else's, probably) to make
himself rich, and instead had made himself and his back-
ers poorer. He probably had plans for lots of houses back
here in the woods, each on a dead-end road with speed
bumps, each one snazzier than the next. But as had happened to more than one land developer on the Vineyard,
his plans had gone awry, and all there was to show for
his dreams were these overgrown dirt roads.

Denise's voice cut through the darkness. "You said
you haven't told the cops anything."

"Not yet."

"I don't want them on my case. I'll tell you whatever
you want to know, but I don't want the cops on my case.
How many other people know what you know? How

many other people do I have to worry about?"

"A girl died in my driveway. That's why I'm here. I'm not a cop. I got into this thing because of the girl. Your friend Kathy. If she'd died somewhere else, I wouldn't be here, but she died on my land. I found out she had a hundred thousand dollars in her checking account and it all ended up in a bank over in Hyannis. The same thing is true of you. Women your age don't generally have that kind of money in their checking accounts. And if they do, they don't work in places like the Fireside."

"How'd you find all this out?"

"Luck and a long nose. Besides, money makes noises that a lot of people eventually hear. Two hundred thousand dollars may not be a fortune to John D. Rockefeller, but it is to most people. It's hard to move that kind of money around and not have anybody find out about it, so I think that whoever is running this particular scam is pretty good, because so far he hasn't gotten himself arrested. Maybe he never will be. Anyway, now I want to hear your side of it."

"It's a long story."

"It's a long night." She didn't say anything. I was conscious of my sore back. After a while I said, "All right, let me tell you what I think, then you can tell me how wrong I am and what's really going on."

"Don't bore me."

I looked at her through the darkness. She was holding her purse in her lap with both hands. Her knees were together, and she was looking at me. Her face was dim and cold.

"Stop me when you've had enough. I think that Glen Gordon is in the middle of it. He's a math and computer guy, and after college he got a job with Frazier Information Services, an outfit that does accounts for a lot of businesses including banks. He's a good worker and soon became very trusted. Since a lot of banks are converting to their own computer systems these days, they don't need FIS to do that work for them anymore, so FIS guys work with bank guys to help transfer accounts to the new system.

"I imagine that Gordy did that sort of work down in New York and was good at it. I think he probably started thinking about how to steal some money while he worked there, but, being the systematic type, took his time setting things up. Getting identity papers for himself and the people he'd need to help him, and that sort of thing. Probably he got the ID's the usual way: checked for deaths in the paper, then later sent for copies of the birth certificates of the dead people and used them to get drivers' licenses, Social Security cards, and the other ID stuff that he'd need.

"Before he went to work for FIS, he had a fling with you. And then, a couple of years later, another one with Kathy Ellis. Told her he was still in college, so she wouldn't get her folks worrying about their little girl getting involved with an older man, I imagine. Anyway, both of you fell pretty hard for him, I figure. Kathy Ellis, at least, was the loving sort who would do anything for her man. Not a bad deal if you're the kind of guy who likes a love slave, and a very good deal if you needed a couple of people who'd do anything for you, even shady stuff. His only problem was that you and Kathy were both going to be working on the Vineyard during the summers. What to do?

"Well, God works in mysterious ways his wonders to perform. One day Gordy hears from a guy working on the Cape that the Vineyard Haven National Bank is going to convert to its own computer system. The guy wants to come to New York, and Glen wants to get close to his girls and to the bank. FIS, being the flextime sort of place it is, makes it easy for the guys to trade places.

"Now Gordy's got everything he needs: a gang, a bank, and the ID's to hide the money trail. He sets up a company called the New Bedford, Woods Hole and Nantucket Salvage Company, with Cecil Jones as its treasurer and a woman named Marilyn Grimes as Jones's assistant. They're both authorized to take money out of the company checking account at the Zimmerman National Bank, over in Hyannis. Jones is actually Gordy himself, more or less in disguise. He probably learned about makeup when he used to do theater work in college, just like you and Kathy Ellis did. As a matter of fact, that's where Gordy met you both. In college theater.

"Anyway, once Gordy had a legitimate account where he could put money he planned to steal, he had you and Kathy Ellis open checking accounts at the Vineyard Haven National Bank. You were both glad to go along with him because he told you there was no way you'd ever get caught, because you loved him and would do anything for him, and because you were both going to make some money that you needed, more money than you can earn bartending in the Fireside, for sure.

"When everything was ready, Gordy got to work on the transfer of accounts to the bank's new computer system. He was a ringtailed wonder, often working alone all night long, supposedly so he could take advantage of FIS's flexplan system to get beach days off, but really so he'd be left alone to do his business with the accounts.

"What he did, I think, was something that he could only do when these sorts of account transferals take place. I think it was probably the only time one person would have access to all the computer systems, including the security systems that would normally prevent people from getting into unauthorized files. It worked something like this."

I tried to remember what Matt Jung and Helen Fine had told me. "The system they're using is called Demand Deposit Accounting. Every customer has an account number and a balance is maintained in that account. If a check is cashed, the money is subtracted from the account and if a deposit is made, money is added. Everything has to balance.

"Now here's the interesting part. Customer accounts are split up into cycles of about a thousand accounts each, and the cycle, like individual accounts, has to balance. If it gets out of balance, say by somebody taking money by means other than a legitimate withdrawal, it would be noticed right away. What Gordy did, I think, was to figure a way to shuffle the money from a dormant account with a couple hundred thousand in it to your account and Kathy's. It's not uncommon for a dormant account to have that much money in it, and for the account to be unused for months, so nobody would notice that the money was missing. And because Gordy made sure that your accounts and the dormant account were in the same cycle, the cycle was never out of balance. The only withdrawals were legitimate: the checks that you and Kathy wrote. Since there was supposedly no activity involving the dormant account, the computer didn't pay any attention to it. No wonder, since Gordy was programming it.

"So Gordy put the money in your accounts and you wrote checks and, I imagine, gave them to Gordy, who, as Cecil Jones, deposited them in the salvage company account. A week or so later, after the checks had cleared, he or Marilyn Grimes withdrew the money in cash. *Voilà!* Lots of money for Gordy. How am I doing so far?"

"You're sharp as a tack, you are."

"You want to take it from here?"

"No. You're so smart, you keep going."

"High praise for a man with a permanently unbalanced checkbook. Okay. I think that Gordy probably knew he only had a certain amount of time to get this job done and to disappear with the dough. There'd be an audit, probably, as soon as the transfer was complete. Something like that.

"Anyway, about this time, things began to go wrong. Maybe Kathy Ellis began to get cold feet. That sort of thing happens among thieves. The cops get a lot of people just because other people crack and begin to talk. Anyway, Kathy Ellis ate something she shouldn't have, and Gordy looks like a likely source of whatever it was she ate. But Kathy's death created danger that wasn't there before, since an odd death always interests the police, and once the police start to nose around, they begin to find out things. Anyway, I figure that Gordy decided he couldn't afford to wait the time it would normally take to have you write checks in amounts less than ten thousand dollars, the kind that don't attract the government's eye, but to have you write the big one for a hundred thou. You did and he deposited it.

"I think maybe he told you to bring it over to him in person, so he wouldn't have to go to the island. I think maybe that's why you pulled your disappearing act. You say you were in New Bedford with a new lover. Maybe so, and maybe if you were, it saved your life since you were just another girl who knew too much. I know that I, at least, was worried about you being the next one to die. When I told you at the bar that I was glad to see you back, I was telling you the truth."

"Gee, a smart guy who's nice, too. Lucky me."

"Once Gordy had the second hundred thou in his salvage company account, all he had to do was wait for the check to clear, draw out the cash, and disappear. He got a jump start on the disappearing part by working nights so he could get four days off, presumably to go to Boston to a rock concert. But there's no rock concert in Boston this weekend, which means that after Marilyn Grimes drew out the cash yesterday, Gordy and Marilyn probably split with the money. Or maybe he split from Marilyn, too. Or maybe Marilyn is lying in the woods someplace on Cape Cod.

"Or, to be fair, maybe none of this happened. Maybe I'm just full of shit." I turned to look at her. "What do you think? Any additions or deletions? Any editing or criticism? Speak up. The podium is yours."

"I'll tell you one thing," she said. "You may think you're a smart bastard, but you're more stupid than smart."

In the dim light, I saw that Denise had a hand in her purse and was fumbling around. When her hand came out, there was a small revolver in it. She aimed it at me and shot me in the stomach.

▪ 26 ▪

I was rising when the bullet hit, and I felt as if I had been struck in the belt buckle by a hammer. I fell backward over the log, spilling the flashlight from my hand. I heard another shot, but it passed above me as I fell. I remember thinking very clearly that Denise must have been blinded by the muzzle flash of the first shot.

I hit the ground and rolled away as Denise shot again. She should have taken her time, but like some other killers she was overanxious. I was afraid I'd be too weak to escape her, but when I tried to get up I succeeded beyond my dreams. I was on my feet in an instant and running into the trees. She fired after me, but it's very hard to hit someone with a pistol when you're impatient and the night is dark. I was instantly in the trees, branches whipping at my eyes, clutching at my clothes.

I stopped running and got a hand to my belly, feeling for the wound, for blood. Instead, I touched the revolver I'd stuck in my belt, and I felt a surge of joy, knowing immediately what had happened: her bullet had hit the pistol. I pulled out the old .38, thumbed the hammer, and rolled the cylinder. It still worked.

My belly ached, and I felt sick, but I had no time for such concerns. I looked back toward the clearing and, very dimly, could see Denise at the log, searching the ground with her hands. I knew what she was after: the flashlight. I eased away through the trees, circling to my right. Behind me, the flashlight suddenly went on, illuminating the trees into which I had run. The light swung first one way, then the other, as Denise listened for my movement. I stopped.

When I saw the flashlight move, I moved again, still circling to the right. When the light moved, I moved. When it stopped, I stopped. As the light went into the trees, I moved out of them, coming into the clearing behind the Land Cruiser. I stuck the .38 back under my belt, knelt, and ran my hands over the ground. I came up with an empty beer can and beer bottle. The light bobbed through the trees. I went to the far side of the Land Cruiser and eased the door open, glad, for once, that the interior light didn't work.

In the trees, the light swept first one way, then the other. I threw the beer can as far as I could in front of the Land Cruiser, and it landed with a satisfying clatter. The light swung in that direction and began to bob forward. I waited until it reached the edge of the clearing, then threw the bottle in the same direction as the can. The bottle clinked nicely, and the light went rapidly out into the clearing. I pulled out the .38, and when the flashlight was forty feet or so in front of the Land Cruiser, I flipped on the headlights. Then I dropped to the ground.

Denise was in the center of the lights, little revolver in one hand, flashlight in the other. She spun toward the truck.

I yelled, "I've got a gun, Denise! Toss that pistol away, or I'll shoot you!"

A good yell will stop some people cold. But not Denise. Instead, she pointed the gun and her light at my voice and fired. I heard the bullet sing off the hood of the Land Cruiser. "Try that trick on somebody else," she said, and came trotting toward me.

"Put down the gun and stay where you are!" I yelled.

"What an incredible asshole you are," she said. "You're even stupider than Gordy was, even stupider than that bitch Kathy."

I had time to aim, so I shot her in the right thigh. The

bullet knocked her leg from under her and spun her around so that she hit the ground very heavily. A grunt exploded from her lungs, and the revolver and flashlight flew from her hands. She grabbed at her thigh and blood began to stream out between her fingers. Moans and oaths mixed in her mouth as tears burst from her eyes.

I went out and picked up the flashlight and pistol, then got on the C.B. and called for the cops and an ambulance. By the time they got there, I had a pressure bandage on the wound, and Denise was feeling the pain. I told the O.B. cops what had happened, and gave them the guns involved. While some of the cops went with Denise to the hospital, the sergeant, who had stayed behind, leaned forward and flashed his light on me. I looked down and saw that there was blood on my clothes and legs.

"I think that some of that's yours," said the sergeant.

So they took me to the hospital, too.

After I was nicely bandaged, I went to the O.B. police station. By that time, Corporal Dominic Agganis of the State Police had showed up, not too pleased at having been routed out of bed at that time of night, and I got to give my statement all over again. Then I got the guys to take me back to my Land Cruiser, so I could drive home. It was getting pretty late.

Not too late for Quinn and Dave, though. They heard me come in, and came out of their bedroom, in ill humor.

"Where the hell have you been?" asked Quinn, rubbing his eyes.

I was hurting and feeling out of sorts. "Who are you? My mother?"

Then Dave noted my bloody clothes, and nudged Quinn.

"Jesus," said Quinn, suddenly wide awake. "What happened to you?"

"Some bullet fragments. Scratches, mostly. More blood than damage."

Quinn's reporter's eyes lit up. "You need some coffee," he said. "Dave, get us some coffee. J. W., you come right over here and sit down. That's right, that's right. Now, start from the beginning."

When I was done, Quinn looked at Dave. "My boy," he said. "I think I'll delay my return to Boston till tomorrow afternoon so I can talk to some cops in the morning. There's a story here with meat on its bones. Murder on Martha's Vineyard. Poison, a shootout at midnight, two hundred grand. Great stuff! I'll give it to the *Globe* and then maybe to the *Inquirer*. Hey, if I mix you into the plot, I can probably sell it to the movies."

Dave nodded. "I can see it. Overworked musician flees fame for R and R on renowned resort island. Discovers nefarious plot, saves the world, and returns to the concert stage as combined pianist and secret agent."

"You got it," said Quinn. "Blockbuster film followed by the spinoff TV series showing musician performing onstage in a different international city every week and solving crimes between concerts in secret agent persona. A different beautiful location and girl every week. Great classical music combined with travel, sex, and violence. Something for every kind of brow, high, middle, or low."

Dave clapped his hands with feigned enthusiasm. "Great! Who do you think we should cast as me?"

"Me," said Quinn. "We can use your hands for the close-ups of the keyboard, but I'll do the rest. I have the face and form of a hero."

"I think I'll go to bed while you two work out the details," I said, and did.

The phone rang at seven the next morning. It was Zee. Her voice was full of alarm.

"What's this about you getting shot? Are you okay?"

"How did you find out about that?"

"I work at the hospital, remember? I have friends there and there's no way you can go up there and be treated for a gunshot and me not learn about it. Are you okay?"

"Of course I'm okay. I didn't really get shot. I only

got nicked by some fragments. Besides, it was only a .22."

"Only a .22, eh? Aren't you the one who thinks that .22's probably kill more people than all of the .45's, 9mm's, 357 Magnums, and all the other guns combined?"

It sounded like something I might say, so I said, "Maybe."

"I'm coming right over!"

The phone clicked in my ear.

I debated whether it would be better for me to get dressed and look manly, or to crawl back into bed and look pitiable. I wasn't sure about manly, but I knew pitiable wouldn't work very well, so I got dressed. As I did, I noticed something. My back didn't hurt. I was sore where the fragments of the bullet had cut me, but my back felt fine. From falling off the log? From having had something more immediate to worry about, like being shot to death, so that the back problem disappeared because by comparison it wasn't worth thinking about? Had it all been in my head? Who knew? Who cared? I was happy.

Out in the living room Quinn was already on the phone. He saw me, covered the speaker with a hand and said, "I'm talking to some people at the *Globe*. Guess what?"

"What?"

"That dead guy in the Drago Hotel? His name's been released. Your friend Glen Gordon. Shot with a .22. I think we'd better tell the O.B.P.D. that they might have the murder weapon in their possession."

"Good idea." Things were falling into place, and a lot of them were piling up on Denise Vale.

When Zee arrived, Maria was with her. Zee's eyes were red. She came to me and put her arms around me and put her head against my chest. I held her tight.

Maria studied her daughter, then stepped close and looked up at me. "Is this what Zeolinda can expect from you? Worry and trouble all the time? Never knowing what will happen to you? Is this the kind of life you plan to give her?"

Zee jerked away from me and whirled toward her mother. "Shut up, Mom! You just be quiet!"

Maria's eyes opened wide.

"Now, Zee," I said. "Your mom's just worried about you . . ."

Zee spun back. "You too, Jefferson! You just close your mouth! I don't want any more of this 'now, Zeolinda, dear' stuff from either of you or anybody else! I never want to hear it again! I know what I want!"

She hugged me again, and I looked over her head at her mother. Maria gazed at her only daughter, then shook her head, and said, "Here I am, acting just like my mother did when I told her I was going to marry your daddy. And there you are, acting just like I did. God preserve us all." Then she smiled an ironic smile, stepped forward, and put her arms around us both. I hooked an arm around her, and after a while Zee did the same. The three of us stood there for quite a time.

By noon, Quinn had made his calls, and we thought we had figured out a lot of what had happened. Zee and Maria were a patient audience as we gave them our theories.

"The mistake I made," I said, "was figuring Glen Gordon for the really bad apple in the barrel, when all the time it was Denise Vale. Glen was a con man and a thief, but he wasn't a killer. It was Denise, not Glen, who killed Kathy Ellis. Denise and Kathy met at Kathy's house and Kathy was never very happy afterward. My guess is that Kathy was having second thoughts about the scam and Denise was trying to put some starch in her spine. When Denise realized that Kathy was really going to spill the beans, she slipped her some water hemlock. Not a bad ploy, all in all, considering Kathy's dietary habits. Hard to prove it was murder even if someone got suspicious. Glen may have thought he was running the show, but Denise was using him from the beginning. I wouldn't be surprised if she planned from the start to keep the money for herself."

Quinn nodded. "And that woman who rented the room in the Drago Hotel where Glen Gordon checked in his chips. The desk clerk thought she was a hooker, but we're willing to bet that the woman was Denise Vale in some other disguise. She'd been an actress in college, remember, so she knew about wigs and makeup and all. And we'll also put money on Denise being Marilyn Grimes." He glanced at me. "Did I tell you that I tracked down the real Marilyn Grimes and the real Cecil Jones? The NYU Alumni Association was glad to give me their addresses. They both live in New Jersey and had no idea that Glen Gordon had borrowed their names."

Zee looked at me. "I thought you didn't recognize Marilyn Grimes when you saw her on the bank's video tape."

"I didn't. She had a false front plate that made her mouth and teeth look different, she wore a wig, and she used makeup to make her look about ten years older than she really was. But once I thought about the two of them being the same person, in my imagination I took off the wig, took out the front plate, scrubbed off the makeup, and, *voilà!* there was Denise Vale. Glen Gordon also wore makeup when he was Cecil Jones, but it wasn't nearly as effective as Denise's."

"The way we figure it," said Quinn, "is that she wanted him to be recognized through his disguise. Of course, she didn't tell him that, but that's what she wanted."

"Why?" asked Zee.

"Because she wanted him to be recognized and take the rap. He was going to be the best kind of fall guy: the dead kind, shot in a cheap Boston hotel room by a hooker the cops could never track down."

"You mean she planned to kill him all along?"

"I don't know about all along, but toward the end she did. She told me that when she left the island she went to New Bedford, but what she really did was go up to

Boston and rent that room at the Drago. Then she had Gordy go up there. He told everybody he was going up to a rock concert, but he was really going up there to meet her and go off with the two hundred thou. Instead, she killed him and took the money for herself."

"I don't get it," said Maria. "Once she had the money and was out of the hotel, why didn't she just take off with it? That's what I would have done."

"Gee, Mom," said Zee. "I didn't know you were so criminally inclined!"

"I'm not," said Maria. "You know what I mean. Why didn't she just leave the country, or go somewhere and take a new name?"

"Because," said Quinn, "if she'd done that, the cops would be looking for her. She funneled a hundred thou through her own checking account, remember. If she'd gone missing, the fuzz would have wanted to talk to her."

"They would have anyway, wouldn't they?"

"Yeah, but what they would have found was a working girl still slinging beer in a local saloon. Quite a different thing from a woman who had disappeared along with two hundred thousand dollars. They would have brought her in and I expect that she would have confessed to having been a fool for letting her boyfriend, that wicked Glen Gordon, exploit her like he did. She would admit that she wrote the check, but claim that she didn't know anything more about how the scheme worked. She might do a little time for her part in the scam, but probably not. Probably the poor used thing would get probation. And probably, after a year or two, she'd go back to New York to live with her mama. And probably after that, she'd disappear into the great American wilderness."

"And what about the money?"

I shrugged. "Ah, the money. I expect that the money is scattered here and there in safety deposit boxes in various banks under various names. In a few years, when Denise was sure the cops weren't watching her very carefully anymore, she would have collected the money. Or maybe she's already invested it in stocks and bonds.''

"But that's not going to happen now. What *is* going to happen?''

"The cops have my testimony about last night, they have the .22 that killed Glen Gordon, and they have a scenario that will allow them to start an investigation of the whole scheme. One thing they might do is check out the room and the phone that was headquarters for the salvage company. Maybe Denise left some fingerprints there. Maybe they can prove that Marilyn Grimes and Denise were the same person. Maybe the desk clerk at the Drago Hotel can identify Denise as the hooker who rented the room where Glen Gordon was killed. Maybe they can find the keys to the safety deposit boxes where Denise is keeping the money until the heat dies down.''

"That's a lot of maybes.''

"The future is spelled M A Y B E. They'll probably get her for assault with a deadly weapon, at least, or maybe even for attempted murder . . .''

"Yours,'' Zee said.

"Mine,'' I agreed. "I think they may get her for killing Glen Gordon, too. Murder, maybe. Manslaughter, maybe, since nobody saw it happen.''

"Maybe self-defense,'' said cynical Quinn. "She may get herself a lawyer who'll convince the jury that Gordon tried to kill her before she killed him.''

I nodded. "In fear of her life, as they say.''

Maria shook her head. "This world. It can be so mean and ugly sometimes.''

Zee cocked her head to one side. "What about that hundred thou in my account that got you going on this case?''

"Ah. Well, nobody's perfect, not even our moneyman, Glen Gordon. Your account number is one digit different than Denise Vale's account number. Glen goofed. He punched the wrong number when he moved the money from the dormant account that weekend. But by Sunday night he found the error and corrected it. Still, if he hadn't made the mistake in the first place, I probably never would have started nosing around." I paused and smiled at Zee. "On the other hand, you could argue that if you hadn't been using those eighteen-inch leaders during that bluefish blitz . . ."

"Oh no you don't!" said Zee, holding up a fist. "We're not going to get started on that again!"

I looked at Maria. "Or maybe you're right. Maybe there is a God who keeps an eye on things and gets involved now and then."

She brightened. "You can bet on it. And more times than now and then, too."

David Greenstein came into the room. He looked at Quinn. "The car's all packed up, and we're ready to roll. A little traveling music, please." He walked over to the tape deck, put in a cassette, and punched the play button. Piano music tumbled out of the speakers and filled the air. Something joyful. It sounded like Vivaldi, who must have had a bad day sometime in his life, but never showed it in his compositions. The music filled the room, gay, lovely, and pure.

Maria listened a moment, then read the title on the cassette container. *David Greenstein in Carnegie Hall.*

We followed Quinn and Dave out to the car. But they were not to leave quite as quickly as they planned. A pickup truck was coming down my long driveway. It stopped in front of Quinn's car, and Miles Vale got out.

"You shot my little girl," he said. "The cops came by last night and told me all about it. I been awake ever since, wondering what to do."

He looked at me with fierce eyes, then reached back into the cab and pulled out a shotgun.

▪ 27 ▪

Zee clutched at my arm, but I pushed her away. She came back, and I pushed her again, so hard that she fell against Dave.

"Hold her," I said. He wrapped his arms around her and pulled her to one side.

"Let me go!" she said, trying to tear his arms away. But he only gripped her tighter. Quinn and Maria stood very still. We all stared at Miles.

He held the shotgun in front of him as though it were a magic wand, and looked first at me, then at the gun, then back at me.

"I been in the house with this thing ever since the cops left," he said, in a dull voice. "I thought that I might shoot you with it. Then I thought I might shoot myself. I been in some scraps in my life, but so far I never shot nobody, not even when I was in the army.

"The cops tell me that my little girl shot you, and that they think maybe she killed some other people, too. How could that be? How could my girl do anything like that? How can people just shoot each other? How could you shoot her?"

I wasn't sure that I should answer, but I did. "I shot her because she'd already shot me once and was trying to shoot me again."

He nodded absently. "The cops said you could have killed her. Maybe you should have, instead of just hurt-

212

ing her. Maybe that would have been better. Now she has to live and know what she did."

I said nothing, thinking that Denise would probably have no trouble living with the knowledge of what she had done.

Miles lifted the shotgun, and studied it. I felt a cold fear in my chest.

"All my life I been a hunter," he said. "I've been a medic, but I've been a hunter, too. I've killed deer and geese and ducks lots of times. Today I thought a long time about killing a human being. I never did that before. I think maybe Denise has more of me in her than I knew I had in myself. She's my daughter, and I love her no matter what she's done, but . . ." He looked right at me. "I'm not going to hunt anymore. Not ever. This is a good gun, but I don't want it in the house."

He leaned the shotgun against the porch, got into his pickup, and drove away.

After a while Dave and Quinn got into Quinn's car.

"Free concert tickets for all, the next time I play in Boston," said Dave in an odd voice.

"You still have to buy your own *Globes*, though," said Quinn.

When they were gone, Maria, Zee, and I went up and sat on my balcony. We didn't have much to say.

Overhead, the summer sky was blue and cloudless. Beyond my garden the tyro surf sailors were learning their skills on the safe, shallow waters of Sengekontacket Pond. Beyond them, along the barrier beach, parked cars already lined the road and the June People had raised their bright umbrellas and spread their blankets upon the sand. There were kites in the air, and on the blue waters of the sound, sailboats were leaning through the wind.

From the door and windows of my house, David Greenstein's joyful music poured forth, danced across my lawn, and lifted past us toward the treetops, toward the heavens, where Maria's mysterious God brooded over his creation.